Billancourt Tales

ALSO BY NINA BERBEROVA

The Book of Happiness *(novel)*
Cape of Storms *(novel)*
The Ladies from St. Petersburg *(three novellas)*
The Tattered Cloak *(stories)*

NINA BERBEROVA

Billancourt Tales

Translated from the Russian with an Introduction by
MARIAN SCHWARTZ

A NEW DIRECTIONS BOOK

Manufactured in the United States of America
Book design by Sylvia Frezzolini Severance
New Directions Books are printed on acid-free paper.
First published in France as *Chroniques de Billancourt* in 1992,
and originally titled *Biankurskie prazdeniki*.

First published clothbound by New Directions in 2001
Published simultaneously in Canada by Penquin Books Canada, Ltd.

Library of Congress Cataloging-in-Publication Data

Berberova, Nina Nikolaevna
    [Biankurskie prazdniki. English]
    Billancourt tales / Nina Berberova ; translated from the
Russian with a preface by Marian Schwartz.
        p.   cm.
    ISBN 0-8112-1481-8 (clothbound : alk. paper
    I. Schwartz, Marian. II. Title.
    PG3476.B425 B55132001
    891.73'42—dc21   2001042583

New Directions Books are published for James Laughlin
by New Directions Publishing Corporation
80 Eighth Avenue, New York 10011

Contents

Introduction

Nina Berberova became known throughout the world only in the last decade of her long life, as novellas like *The Accompanist* and *The Tattered Cloak* began to appear in translation. With the coming of *glasnost*, her fame grew in Russia, where her biography of Moura Budberg in particular won her a place among the essential Russian writers of the twentieth century.

But this came after—after eighty years of relative obscurity during which she produced a steady stream of history, criticism, reportage, biography, and autobiography, as well as fiction and poetry. Born in St. Petersburg in 1901 and progressively educated, she had grown up to despise the tsar and to embrace the "modern." The 1917 Russian Revolution caught her while she was completing her education and making her first public attempts at writing. As a child and adolescent, Berberova had always imagined herself a writer; she hadn't imagined, however, that she would spend her entire writing career in exile, separated from her principal audience.

In 1922, Berberova left Russia with the last fleeing group of
intellectuals, including her lover, the poet Vladislav
Khodasevich. The couple, however, did not reach Paris, the
intellectual center of the Russian emigration, until 1925. Upon
their arrival, Berberova immediately began working for the lib-
eral democratic Russian émigré newspaper, *The Latest News*
(*Poslednie novosti*), where she published articles and short stories.
In her preface to the French edition of the *Billancourt Tales*,
Berberova explained her initial dilemma:

> I began writing fiction in 1925, and for two years I
> sought a ground, or a base, or a background, where my
> heroes could live and act. I hadn't had time to know Old
> Russia, and even if I had, I wasn't interested in writing
> about it. There were quite enough "old" writers in the
> emigration (and in its center, Paris) who could use their
> memories of tsarist Russia only to entertain those who
> lived in the past. It never occurred to me to write about
> France or French "heroes," as some beginning fiction
> writers my age did. I could have started writing about
> myself, of course, as did many young writers in the
> West then, on Proust's example, but at the time I was
> incapable of speaking or writing about myself. I had to
> find—to at least some small extent—an established
> everyday setting and people who had settled in one
> place, if not permanently then at least for the time
> being, and who had created a semblance of ordinary life,
> regardless of whether I liked the situation they had cre-
> ated or even whether I liked them.

It was two years before Berberova came up with a solution:
Billancourt, an in-lying suburb of Paris located between the
Seine and the Bois de Boulogne, where Renault hired Russian

refugees to build automobiles. After the last battles of the Civil War were fought and the Bolsheviks had established Soviet power throughout Russia, the remnants of Russia's White Army had fled to the Princes Islands, Bizerta, Bulgaria, Serbia, and elsewhere to await their fate. Because these men were healthy and could be easily assimilated into the French population, the manufacturing and agriculture industries decided to bring them to France to reconstitute the work force that had been decimated in World War I. Large and small enclaves of these "White" Russians grew up all over France, the largest one being centered around the Renault plant in Paris.

> Not until 1927 did I find out that the "Russian masses" could be seen on Sundays in the Russian church. I went there and was amazed at the number of people (a full church, a crowd in the churchyard), the overwhelming majority of them men—and even some little children, but a total absence of school-age children and adolescents. I also found out there were churches in the suburbs (which we began calling the "forty forties"*), and that there were suburbs where there were not only churches but also stores, and Russian signs, and a Russian kindergarten, and Sunday schools. Russian holidays were observed there in the old style; certain Russian committees made strenuous efforts on behalf of the old men and invalids from the world war. And in Billancourt there were ten thousand Russians building Renault automobiles.

Billancourt became Berberova's "established everyday setting," and the "Russian masses" of Billancourt became the char-

---

* After a standard epithet for the churches of Moscow—Trans.

acters of Berberova's newspaper stories, which she called "fiestas." In these tales, "Perekop"—the isthmus connecting the
Crimea to Ukraine where in 1920 the Red Army decisively
defeated Wrangel in the Russian Civil War—becomes short-
hand for their defeat, and the scarcity of women (not allowed to
immigrate to France because not considered useful labor) repre-
sents a crisis for these lonely men. These workers were "people
without language, torn from their native soil without hope of
ever returning, who had lost their loved ones and been tossed
out into Europe after military defeat." Because they were not
French citizens, they had only their own to look to in time of
need. *Billancourt Tales* consists of thirteen of the stories about
life in Billancourt that Berberova wrote between 1928 and
1940, as she simultaneously began to write more mature novellas and novels like *The Tattered Cloak*, *The Ladies from St.
Petersburg*, and *The Book of Happiness*.

Berberova was the first to recognize these as relatively simple stories from the standpoint of style and structure. The characters all inhabit one world. It's not hard to imagine them—
some show up in several stories—passing each other on the
street or brushing shoulders in the lobby of the Hotel Caprice.
They share a world view: we have lived through terrible times;
we have seen (and lost) everything; we may dream occasionally,
but we are never surprised when those dreams don't pan out.
Her characters pay lip service to modest lives and humble ambi-
tions, so we assume these people are merely meek. Yet their pas-
sions—love, fear, longing—seethe. A would-be actor blows his
chances at a movie career because he is too law-abiding to act
the part of a thief. A piano player gives up his bookkeeping job
to play in a movie house only to be sent back to bookkeeping by

the theater owner's decision to "modernize." A modest inventor convinces a successful émigré to patent his new idea, but before the deal is settled, the financier dies. When a young man dies and leaves a manuscript among his possessions, his best friends discover he had hidden aspirations as a writer. There is very little longing for Russia in these stories. Rather, the characters of Billancourt are coping with the personal consequences of their disrupted lives: lovers lost, lovers never found; children acquired haphazardly, children estranged out of pure spite; the impossibility of ever truly fitting in.

Berberova's stated attitude toward her characters—who were also her readers—was necessarily ironic: "I don't know whether my readers understood the irony of my stories, whether they were aware that God only knows what kind of 'fiestas' they had in that life of theirs, that between me and my 'heroes' lay an abyss—in way of life, background, education, chosen profession, to say nothing of political views." In Berberova, irony did not become ridicule, however. Berberova may have been wholly of the intelligentsia, and Billancourt was certainly not her world, but she knew a thing or two about poverty. She had spent her entire adult life so far (and would spend three decades more) in Russia, Europe, and the United States, in severely straitened circumstances which would not improve significantly until she began her teaching career in the United States.

In emigration, the Russian language was doomed to diverge from its source and ultimately disappear. Berberova was acutely aware of how distinctive the language had already become. In Paris, Russian changed not only by absorbing French words, sometimes refashioning them into Russian (*photozhenikh* from *photogénique*), but in other ways as well, becoming "more colorful, less unified." It incorporated words picked up from Soviet newspapers or from occasional visitors from Soviet Russia—words like *spets* (specialist), *shamat'* (eat), and *baranka* (automobile), which quickly dropped out of use in the homeland but hung on among the "Whites." The émigrés were having to come up with names for things which had never existed before, "words hastily concocted in the editorial offices of Russian newspapers for translations from French," until they learned and adopted the word established in Russia. Finally, some purely French words were appropriated that remained French. One sees all these influences in the original Russian texts, snapshots of a brief and exotic linguistic era.

Berberova modeled her Billancourt tales after the example of Mikhail Zoshchenko, a popular contemporary writer who maintained a similarly skeptical and ironic outlook, although he, unlike Berberova, directed it toward the aspirations of the Soviet state. Zoshchenko was a master of the *skaz*, a peculiarly Russian genre that involves exactly the same device we see in the *Billancourt Tales*: the contrast between the narrator's voice (Grisha) and everyone else. It is an old-fashioned device that Berberova well understood but later renounced:

> In about 1931, in parallel with the *Billancourt Fiestas*, I began writing stories in my own voice, rejecting the narrator device, and in 1934 I freed myself from the narrator entirely. But this was the end of the *Billancourt Fiestas*. Without a narrator they could not exist. Another period began, perhaps less interesting sociologically but undoubtedly more mature artistically, which led me to my later stories of the 1940s and

1950s, in which I am now fully responsible for both the
irony and the entire basic position of the author-narra-
tor. And where the heroes of the stories are not people
I observe attentively and cautiously, but the déclassé
intellectuals among whom I lived and with whom I
identified.

Although Berberova came to view her Billancourt "fiestas"
as of purely sociological interest, the reader will likely conclude
that she was wrong. Today, it seems she was too hard on the narrator device, which she used deftly and sparely. These are
accomplished genre pieces based on a fascinating world now
gone. Readers familiar with Berberova will instantly realize
something else as well: that she injected something of herself in
the narrator-character of Grisha, a (failed) writer. Berberova's
irony is filtered through but not applied to her narrator.
Grisha's point of view informs the reader. Grisha's recurrence
helps create the sense of Billancourt as a single, integral world.
He indicates where the irony lies and sets the tone not of
ridicule but of compassion. Berberova may have been "incapable
of speaking about herself" directly, but she let something very
personal creep in here.

If Grisha is in fact her alter ego (if so, it would not be the
last time Berberova invested her own perspective in a male character), in him Berberova shows us a side of herself and a view of
the world that do not come out anywhere else in her writing,
not even in her autobiography, where Berberova seems never to
have questioned her abilities or her decisions. No matter how
many obstacles life threw up, she never wondered how to sur-
mount them. Grisha, on the other hand, for all his writerly

detachment and ironizing, is frank about his self-doubt. If his own world has been snatched away and his new world is so precarious, how can he ever become a real writer? This feels like a glimpse of Berberova in her bathrobe, before she has combed her hair and put on makeup—before her guard is up. Grisha's affect rings true in a way that, say, that of the protagonist in *The Book of Happiness*, a novel which draws heavily on the events of Berberova's life, does not. In the narrator of these obscure stories, which were not collected in a book until sixty years after their original publication, Berberova may have given us a rare and candid insight into her private struggle. The *Billancourt Tales* surprise the reader with another clue to the Berberova puzzle.

—Marian Schwartz

Billancourt Tales

Billancourt Fiesta

It was the national holiday on the Place Nationale. The evening of July 14th.

A stage had been set up where our people usually sit at sunset twiddling their thumbs, or stroll, chatting. On it was a four-man orchestra that had been engaged to play the same waltz all night long. The drum beat sad and loud, couples swirled, a thick wall of people watched from the sidelines; there was plenty to look at.

This time the couples were the genuine article, each cavalier dancing with his lady; occasionally you'd come across two cavaliers, of course, but rarely, and no one paid them any mind.

The local lion danced (I never did find out how this lion earned his living). A Chinaman danced, a swoop of hair carefully trained over his right eye; my boss, my foreman (a member of the French Communist Party, actually), wearing sky blue suspenders, danced.

The rest of the politically unaffiliated public, with some Arabs interspersed, were standing in a circle, arms hanging at their sides.

There were many precious and even priceless faces in that crowd, shaven not only because of the national holiday but also because it was Sunday. Parts ran across heads like bright shoelaces, took a turn eight and a half centimeters above the ear and, rounding the crown in a free line, descended to a starched collar. The starched collar that dug into the neck was clean as a whistle, something you couldn't say about the tie, which twisted and turned for no apparent reason on the chest of someone who had already suffered more than his share. A vest of a blue so dark it was almost black, nipped in at the waist by a tailor's invisible stitch, often swathed such a chivalrous form you couldn't help but feel a certain pride for the vest's wearer. The cleaned boots and colorfully patterned socks were less visible by dint of the twilight. The most priceless faces, as always, were rather pale and puffy from their cares and God only knows what nutrition. Even on a holiday you saw no happy satiety in them; what mostly showed through were their nerves. Individuals walked around the square, to and fro, watching the dancing. The sky was growing dark, the apartment buildings shrouded in the evening's gray. The drum beat sad and fine.

There were three of us—Shchov, Petrusha, and me—sitting under a high canvas awning lettered "Cabaret." Petrusha—my dear friend Peter Ivanovich, actually—simply could not come to any agreement with Shchov, who'd fought alongside him, concerning where they both were at dawn on December 23, 1919. And if it was on that side of B., the famous fortress, then why wasn't Colonel Maimistov with them? Their argument had dragged on since morning with only brief respites.

"Grisha, tell him!" Petrusha—Peter Ivanovich, that is—shouted at me. "Why don't you say something? Tell him he was drunk that day so his memories have flitted away like moths. Because if we really had been on that side, Maimistov wouldn't have been away at headquarters, that stubborn soul, he would have been right there with us like the most inseparable friend."

"I was not drunk," Shchov replied. "I mean, I couldn't have been drunk because it was Wednesday."

"Wednesday! Dear God, now he really has lost his mind. Grisha, believe me, it was Monday! Why don't you say something?"

Why did they have to hash out every detail of the distant past? He, Petrusha, Peter Ivanovich, that is, later admitted to me that he wanted to write a military history, even if he only printed three copies, for God's sake: one for himself, one for posterity, and one for the woman he loved, should she ever come his way. Shchov was only annoying him as a matter of course.

Just then, a vision appeared from around the corner. It was wearing a sky blue, knee-length silk dress and a sky blue hat; it was holding a brown leather purse. Head held high, it walked past the three of us toward the dancing. Everyone turned to look. It lingered in the crowd, shifting from foot to foot, and suddenly evaporated before our very eyes: it had gone to dance with the local lion to the waltz the reader has already heard all about.

A mere scrap of blue hat flashed by. The crowd of spectators was getting thicker and thicker, and the drum was beginning to fill them with longing.

"That's it! That's it!" Petrusha shouted when we lost the scrap of hat entirely. "Right this minute my entire life's happiness may have gone to dance, and simpleton that I am, I'm sitting here wondering about Colonel Maimistov. What I'd like is

a better fit between my emotional behavior and the circumstances of my life."

"Often there is no fit," said Shchov. "Why should there be?
You don't think it comes from living a good life, do you?"

Neither one of us had anything to say.

"If you want a fit, go dance: it's the national holiday on the
Place Nationale, the band is playing. . . . What are you sitting
here for?"

But we didn't dance.

"You know, Shchov, you've got it all wrong again,"
exclaimed Petrusha. "I say you have to try as hard as you can."

"It's not in our nature."

He was taller than both of us, and he must have been able
to see the blue hat because he glanced in that direction much
too often.

"The drum's playing. If you're not going to dance, at least
you should walk around and look at the others. Or else what?"

Petrusha stood partway up again and searched with his
eyes. In the crowd I finally saw the ethereal dress and the brown
purse in the small hand. The vision was waving her handkerchief. Not one of us took his eyes off her. We didn't feel like
talking about December 23, 1919, anymore.

"Hello, Petrusha," said Semyon Nikolaevich Kozlobabin
the businessman as he walked up to us. "Isn't that your car
parked on the corner? How about making some honest money
by driving me to the Gare du Nord and back? I have to meet
my brother."

Kozlobabin the businessman looked troubled. He had tied
a silk kerchief around his neck and put on a raincoat, even
though the night was practically hot.

"Are you still celebrating? Then I beg your pardon, I'll find someone else. Perhaps the captain is at liberty?"

Shchov didn't answer. Petrusha said: "Oh, why not, I'll go."

Semyon Nikolaevich Kozlobabin looked at his watch.

"I want to meet my weak-chested brother," he repeated without any special enthusiasm. "We haven't seen each other in nine years."

Petrusha went to start up the motor. He couldn't just leave, though: he got out of the car and walked over to me.

"Can I ask you one favor, Grisha?" he said. "Watch her, brother, the one in the blue with the purse, see who she goes with and where. Got it?"

I didn't blink. "Fine, Petrusha my boy, I'll watch her."

As he was getting in the car, Semyon Nikolaevich Kozlobabin said to me: "Would you like to come for a ride with us, Grigory Andreevich? There's room. You might get various impressions: you might see a train or someone might get run over. Isn't that the sort of thing you like? Maybe some interesting idea will occur to you."

Again, I didn't blink. "No, I'm very grateful, but life's too short to go chasing after ideas. I'd rather sit here with the captain."

Shchov and I were left in our seats and our silence.

It was growing dark. The calvados in our glasses was dispersing its fragrance. The dance circle was getting rowdy.

"Why does our businessman seem less than overjoyed at seeing his brother?" Shchov, asked. "He should be jumping up and down, hugging every friend and stranger he meets, but he's his usual self."

"So the way he's acting doesn't fit the moment."

"Exactly."

"You know, though, Captain, I might not be doing exactly what I ought to right now either. Maybe I have reason to hate someone but I'm just not saying anything."

He gave me an astonished look.

"And maybe," he said significantly, "maybe I have reason right now to start a fight."

"You mean you don't always find yourself fitting the circumstances either."

He looked as if he had just remembered something. He pushed his cap back on his head and wiped his sweaty forehead with the palm of his hand. He eyed me as if he were unsure of something, as if he had definite doubts.

"Swear to me, Grisha, swear you'll never tell anyone this, no matter how hard things get for you, no matter how bankrupt."

"Well, would you listen to that!"

"Swear."

"And just where am I supposed to go telling anyone? What am I, a writer or something? Who do you take me for? And how long can they put me away for this?"

"So you'll swear?"

What could I do! I swore. He began his story, and for a while I forgot all about the blue hat.

"It happened ages and ages ago. I was twenty-eight years old and married—not to Maria Sergeevna, to Maria Fyodorovna still, who ran off with Lieutenant Tsarsky in that very first year of our marriage and later died in childbirth in Bakhmut, at 3 Sadovy Lane.

"At the time, that is, the time I'm telling about, we were

young newlyweds living on Gorshevaya Street, not Sadovy Lane. We lived with Maria Fyodorovna's father, my father-in-law, Fyodor Petrovich—his last name was Petrov, too.

"Which is to say that we were managing. My father-in-law was a retired staff captain, though in all his days he'd never seen combat—he'd had that great good fortune, not like you and me. But my father-in-law loved to tell stories about military life. We'd be sitting there on a holiday, it would be dusk, and my father-in-law would be so wrapped up in talking about maneuvers you could never cut him off. He walked with a cane and was striking to look at, quite attractive really. His small capital, all he had, he gave to his daughter Maria Fyodorovna on her wedding day, holding back a mite so he could eat, drink, and wear clean linen. I must say, he was a sweetie pie, not a father-in-law.

"Time flies, though, and my father-in-law was turning sixty-one. One fine spring evening, just as he was getting ready to reminisce about a certain parade, he was taken by a stroke, first his tongue a little, and then it got stronger and stronger through his arms and legs. The next day Fyodor Petrovich was dead.

"Maria Fyodorovna cried a day, a night, and then another day. Truth be told, this dreadful event laid me pretty low, too.

"The house was inundated with aunts of every stripe—fat ones, who mostly rummaged around in the storerooms, and skinny ones, who went for the dresser drawers. Requiems were offered up twice a day and the guests were served heavy food and drink. The deceased lay oh so quietly off by himself in the corner of the room, the same room where his canary always sang, before and after his death.

"The day of the funeral came. It was morning, the sun was shining, the flowers were blooming. People had gathered at the house, the parish clergy, guests. I was standing in our bedroom, wiping my boots with a cloth, all set to go out, but Maria Fyodorovna just couldn't seem to get her veil attached to her hat. She'd torn the veil taking the hat off the shelf (the veil had been sewn on in haste, for another funeral). But she had to get her hat ready because immediately after the prayers came the bearing-out, and there was only a moment, that is, no time to fuss with a veil.

"I was standing in the middle of the room when from outside the window, our open second-story window, I heard from far away someone walking through our quiet streets. In the middle of the day some not entirely sober personage was playing the concertina and singing.

"At first you could barely hear it. At first, that is, there was still hope that this concertina would pass us by, that it would go down another street, the next one. But then the whole crew turned right down Gorshevaya and you could hear the song up and down the street, with its crazy bawling and strumming, the likes of which I've never heard since:

> *If a gentleman has no watch chain*
> *Then the gentleman has no watch.*

"I took a few steps toward the window and saw the singer himself, who dipped with each step, his eyes focused on the sky, his elbows opened all the way out, and the concertina traveling along in his arms. He was trailed by eight or so little boys of indeterminate age who were running, running ahead, running in small circles, laughing. . .

"That watch and chain made me shudder. The song was

coming right up to our windows; the concertina (where did he get it?) was plucking, pulling, exhausting, clattering, flicking, pestering, cudgeling, arranging the notes. I'm sorry, but they really were something special.

"And all of a sudden I couldn't keep it up. I stopped fitting the moment—the deceased and the bearing-out and everything. Right then, unwittingly, who knows why, my shoulders started twitching to the beat. Maria Fyodorovna didn't notice. As I said, she was fixing her veil. She was so preoccupied that quite mechanically, a pin in her mouth, she hummed a few notes and fell silent immediately. Then, placing the hat on her dresser and uttering a soft *tra-la-la*, she took two little steps to one side while tilting her head toward her shoulder.

"I took a cautious step and Maria Fyodorovna looked over her shoulder. Evidently it was getting to her as well, but who else it was getting to I don't know. She stretched both her hands out to me, and at first we trod in place, catching the music with our feet, then we took a few steps between the commode and the sewing machine, and then we launched into a polka around the room along with the concertina:

> *If a young lady wears a corset,*
> *Then the lady has no bust.*

"Suddenly the music broke off. The patrolman on the corner had put an end to it. We stopped, still holding on to one another. Stricken, Maria Fyodorovna collapsed in my arms, which scared me, and my head began spinning. I opened the door wide and dragged my wife out, into the hall—to the seat of honor, ahead of all the aunts. The prayers were starting."

Shchov stopped talking, and I saw his eyes slanting in the same direction as mine. The vision had emerged from the crowd, which in the meantime had become much denser and larger: a button nose, a hat with just a little too much froufrou. She was followed by the local lion threading his way through the crowd. He was carrying her leather purse and his bouton-niere was coming unpinned.

Shchov pushed his cap forward and jumped up:

"I've got to go. I have to. I can't just let this happen."

He took off across the square after them. The drum was beating, tearing at my heart.

Little by little I started recalling the times my own behav-ior hadn't fit, when I'd started to dance just like that, or nearly like that, at the wrong time, all the times I'd led with a six when I should have led with an ace. All the times I'd laughed at the wrong moment and been drunk in front of people who weren't. Or felt like going home to mama when I had my marching orders. Who hasn't had rotten experiences like that! Of course, I'm not talking about foreign citizens, who always do everything at the proper time, naturally.

Then Petrusha's car pulled up right in front of me—at the entrance to the Hotel Caprice actually. Semyon Nikolaevich Kozlobabin the businessman and his weak-chested brother, newly arrived, were getting out. The brother looked to be about fifty and was wearing a dark shirt without any tie, a cap that had gone out of style a long time ago, and an earring. My Petrusha was dragging a pillow out of the automobile—all the weak-chested Kozlobabin had for luggage was this strapped-up pillow and an Easter cake wrapped in newspaper. The weak-chested brother looked all around—the drum was a little intimidat-ing—and kept an eye on Petrusha to make sure he didn't swipe his Easter cake. Semyon Nikolaevich took him by the arm:

"Don't be afraid of the drum, Kolya. It's our national holi-day: the storming of the Bastille. You know better than I, of course, what happened then at that point in history. Brother dear, you need to drink something after your long trip, let a quick shot or a glass of *joie de vivre* slide down your throat. Peter Ivanovich will carry your things straight to the room. Madame will show him where. Everyone knows us well and respects us here. There's really nothing for you to be embarrassed about."

Semyon Nikolaevich the businessman walked over to my table, introduced me to his brother, and sang my praises. They sat down and continued their brotherly conversation:

"So, you're here, that means you tore yourself away to see us, so to speak. . . . My family's gone to the dacha, though, so I'm on my own right now, you understand. I have business here, you know, I just can't get away. But you don't care about that, I'd rather hear about Misha. Is he alive? What about Anna Petrovna? Where are the Kuroyeds? In one piece?"

"Yes."

"Did you see Marusya before you left? Have you had any letters from the Don? Aren't the children going to school already?"

"Yes."

The weak-chested Kozlobabin was sitting there and you could tell he was listening to the drum, looking around, and marveling—and worrying a little. Petrusha walked up and leaned over to me: "Did you see?"

"Yes. They left together and Shchov ran after them. I hope there's no fight. If I were you, I'd pass."

Petrusha bit his lip, sat down, and started listening to the brothers' conversation, too.

I can't lie, they weren't really having a conversation.
Kozlobabin the businessman was peppering his brother with
questions about all sorts of people, plying him with liquor, trying to explain his own material situation. The brother sat perfectly still and silent, shuddering occasionally, wary. He would
look at Petrusha and me as if he could not tear himself away,
then look around at the increasingly noisy celebrants nearby, at
the dancers, the spectators, the lovers, the Chinese chasing each
other, the elegant full-breasted girls from the bread, sausage,
and dairy stores.

On the far corner, where there was another little café which
we zealously avoided, our own musicians announced their presence. They began sawing away at the fiddle and slapping the
bass, and a horn floated over us like honey. As far as I could tell,
the two orchestras were playing completely different pieces
simultaneously.

And something strange started happening to our weak-
chested Kozlobabin brother. He hunched over his glass and hid
his hands under the table, his face turned red, a tear rolled down
his cheek. Very odd.

Semyon Nikolaevich the businessman immediately left off
his familial talk, and the newcomer grew embarrassed and
pulled a handkerchief from his pocket—very slowly. The handkerchief was filthy from his train trip.

"What's wrong, you aren't crying are you?" asked Semyon
Nikolaevich. The newcomer guiltily raised his eyes to Petrusha
and me.

"What's the matter? Look, there's music playing, people are
having a good time, it's a holiday here today. They're dancing.
What's wrong?"

The newcomer looked down at his knees and a second tear crawled down his other cheek.

"Forgive me, comrades," he said quietly. "I'm sorry."

Petrusha blushed and started squirming in his chair. "I humbly beg the comrades to leave him in peace. Our extremist elements might hear and raise a scandal."

The newcomer covered his face with his hands, which after his trip were not like the hands of someone on his way to Easter services. Nor were his nails.

Semyon Nikolaevich was embarrassed. "What an odd fellow you are, Kolya! How I'm supposed to console you, I don't know."

I moved my saucer a little.

"Did you leave some beloved object at home?"

Kozlobabin's weak-chested brother did not reply.

"Did you lose it en route?"

"Does something hurt after your trip?"

"Do you regret spending the money?"

The newcomer didn't answer but kept his hands over his face. It was getting awkward to look at him. Petrusha wouldn't let up.

"Don't you like our national holiday?"

"Are you sorry they aren't dancing like this in Moscow?"

"Or do they dance there every day, whereas here we only dance once a year, and you feel sorry for us?"

He sat there perfectly still without answering, and his glass started trembling slightly on the table. We could not fathom the reason for this disparity between his state of mind and his surroundings.

Still, he wasn't a young man and he was the brother of

Semyon Nikolaevich Kozlobabin, a man of substance whose
wife and daughter had managed to slip away to the dacha. He
was a newcomer, and we were having a holiday on our square,
where some were strolling arm in arm with girls from sausage
stores and others with girls from bakeries. And this lack of fit
between his mood and the waltzers' hadn't been obvious at all.

"We'd better hit the hay," an embarrassed Semyon
Nikolaevich finally said. "It's time you went to bed, little
brother. Traveling's got you down."

The newcomer finally uncovered his face, which was now
perfectly dry, and everyone felt a little better. Kozlobabin took
his brother by the elbow, paid for them both, and they went to
get settled at the Hotel Caprice.

That left Petrusha and me. And once again we saw the
vision. But this time it was walking on Shchov's arm showing
all its pearly teeth as it laughed. Petrusha couldn't stand it and
rushed over to introduce himself. Should I have taken advantage
of the moment, too? But I didn't budge.

I sat there a little longer and listened to both of the hired
orchestras, which were still playing different pieces. Night was
lingering, floating, sailing up—I don't know how else to put it.
And then they set off the fireworks. People started dancing on
the third corner, where they sell oysters and other shellfish in
the winter and where one of ours was plucking on a balalaika.

The crackling fireworks made a pretty show and flew
apart harmlessly in the sky. What children there were
screamed, and the women squinted and tossed their heads
back—as if they knew squinting and tossing their heads back
became them. In the sky, where the moon should have been,
all you could see were green and red sparks. No one gave a

thought to the moon, though, and what could you say about the stars?

It was probably a good thing that Kozlobabin's weak-chested brother had been taken away before any fireworks. If street-lamps could make a man cry, a man tempered in life's battles, then fireworks might have had the devil knows what effect on him. And what man in our day hasn't been tempered in life's battles? For us, there is no such man.

1929

Photogénique

Gerasim Gavrilovich, brother to the Boris Gavrilovich we all know, father of a family, infantryman and worker, was sitting on a bench in the middle of the square, twiddling his thumbs. He didn't feel like going home—it was crowded there and they weren't counting on an extra place for supper. It was a little crowded for him in our small restaurant, too, and most of all—it cost money. So here was the brother of our Boris Gavrilovich sitting and, as I said, frittering away his time.

It was dusk. Couples were strolling. Don't go thinking knights and young ladies, which, due to the dearth of ladies among us, rarely happens. It was just working men strolling, always one tall and one short, for some reason. They fanned themselves from the heat with whatever came to hand, smoked cheap cigarettes, stopped in at the Cabaret, and recalled bygone days and battles where together they had brandished swords.

Truth be told, most were coming down our street to have supper.

Gerasim Gavrilovich was sitting, twiddling his thumbs. The smell of pickles, fruit drops, and fish was coming from the grocer's, where they were lighting the lamp. Kvass was being sold on the corner and an impecunious photographer was lounging on the other. The usual scene.

Gerasim Gavrilovich noticed a copy of the French evening paper under his bench. He picked it up and read it while there was sufficient light. He skipped events in China and the rivalries among deputies, as well as some interesting lawn tennis competitions, and turned straight to the classifieds. In the seven years of his French life, Gerasim Gavrilovich had caught on to reading the employment notices and had even taken a liking to this. He had often had occasion to peruse them, but always somehow with results imperceptible to the unaided eye.

Without the slightest haste or visible agitation, Gerasim Gavrilovich poked the paper with his index finger and tore out a scrap that he stuck in his pocket. And then, as if nothing whatsoever had happened, he made a sour face and moved on to the deputy rivalries, seeing as how his friends and acquaintances wouldn't emerge from the little restaurants until they were well fed and the August night had fallen.

Gerasim Gavrilovich's person had been seen in a number of places: he'd worked on a Greek steamer, in a mine in Belgium, and at a factory in Creusot. How and why he ever ended up here we didn't know. At one time his esteemed brother wanted to teach him his art, but nothing came of it: Gerasim Gavrilovich turned out to have no talent for hairdressing. And his wife was up to her ears in children all day.

"How is it," she used to say to him angrily, "that you, the great Baron von Lazybones, can't make your way anywhere? How is it that God never gave you any talent? Are you planning to live your whole life without a profession of any kind?"

"They pulled the ground right out from under me," Gerasim Gavrilovich would say then. "Your spaces, your seasons, your climates—none of them suit me."

And Boris Gavrilovich, his energetic brother, would deliver his favorite speech about how every person has to know himself. "You," he would say, "you have to know yourself, know which way you're inclined. The ancient Greeks reminded us of this. Sense what's ahead, where your abilities lie: working in a mine or plying the hairdresser's trade. Otherwise, in our day, without a career, you'll be lost. We know all about people who are allowed to do whatever they want!"

Gerasim Gavrilovich left the house early the next morning with the classified in his pocket and headed for the office of a cinematic *société anonyme*. The fact that the company was *anonyme* bothered him a little, but he decided to shrug it off.

The office was located in a spacious film studio. It was noisy on the other side of the wooden barrier. Work was under way, and he could hear chattering, a voice shouting crudely, anything but shy. A man of gloating appearance sat at a desk, and in front of him, silent and melancholy, milling around like sheep, were people who had come in search of work as extras—in crowd scenes or smaller groups—in the new cinematic drama.

The young ladies here were fashionable, completely without eyebrows (there was one with heavy eyebrows, but it turned out she was dreaming of a comic rôle). The browless young ladies jangled their bracelets and earrings and twirled colored scent sticks. Two brigands and one general, all three wearing worn jackets, stuck together. Gilded youths with cheeky ties were taking this free moment to exchange winks with the young ladies. The boss had his own way of dealing with this whole large flock: he would raise his head a fraction to see whether you were going hungry.

Gerasim Gavrilovich walked up to the desk.

"Do you have a tailcoat?" the boss asked. "Do you play soccer? Dance the minuet?"

Gerasim Gavrilovich turned to walk away.

"Stop!" the boss exclaimed. "We might be able to use you. Monsieur (he said a name) needs to look at you."

My God, the envy in the looks the browless young ladies shot Gerasim Gavrilovich! They were all escorted out then and there, the gilded youths along with them. Of the whole throng they held back one brigand. He and Gerasim Gavrilovich sat together for an hour and a half awaiting momentous decisions.

Monsieur (he said the name), wearing a thousand-franc jersey, sweaty, skinny, and good-looking, ran up smoking two cigarettes at once (to make it stronger) and fiddling with a tape measure. He ignored Gerasim Gavrilovich until he had located a big apple in the desk drawer and consumed it on the spot. Then he flung himself down in the armchair (causing a column of dust to rise in the air) and ordered Gerasim Gavrilovich and the brigand to walk back and forth in front of him as if they were strolling across a bridge and admiring the river. Without inquiring about tailcoats or the minuet he led them both past the barrier.

Under the studio's high roof loomed a Spanish town of enviable proportions. Several Spanish caballeros, yawning, were refreshing themselves with sandwiches. A child all made up as Spanish clung to his mother, who was anything but a Spaniard. It was their break time. Two staircases led to the ceiling. There, someone was dangling his legs, probably the lights man, but it might even have been a stuntman. Two painters, one tall and one short, were walking about in leisurely fashion. You weren't supposed to smoke in there.

"Gerasim Gavrilovich, is that you?" exclaimed one of the painters. "My dear man, don't you recognize me? I knew you on the ship, and in Creusot. Have you forgotten Konoteshenko?"

Gerasim Gavrilovich went over to embrace him.

"What are you doing, looking for work? As a painter? A carpenter?"

Gerasim Gavrilovich became flustered.

"I answered an ad for an actor. I'm waiting for a final answer from the bosses."

Konoteshenko, the painter, was awfully pleased.

"Well, they're probably going to give you a shot, to find out whether or not you're *photogénique*. There's luck for you, Gerasim Gavrilovich. Other people spend weeks hanging around before they're told to prop up a set for twenty-two francs a day, but they obviously want to give you a part. Then you'll finally have a career. And it's true, your looks are very suitable, how come you never realized that before?"

Here it should be pointed out that Gerasim Gavrilovich's appearance was nothing like Boris Gavrilovich's. As everyone knows, Boris Gavrilovich is not particularly tall, whereas Gerasim is quite. Boris Gavrilovich greases his hair professionally with petroleum jelly; Gerasim's is shaggy around the ears. Their noses are different, too. One looks like it's made from the crust of a loaf of bread, the other from the soft insides.

Gerasim Gavrilovich perched on a counter in the studio after listening to Konoteshenko. Had his life's path actually led him to a real career? If that wasn't the damnedest thing! Had he really come to know himself, as the ancient Greeks had enjoined? Were the time and the space and the climate finally going to suit him?

For another hour and a half, Gerasim Gavrilovich waited alongside the brigand. The Spanish caballeros went to play billiards. The child was led away. What was happening on the other side of the barrier was a mystery. The tedium was just about to kill Gerasim Gavrilovich when suddenly he and the brigand were told to stand up.

The pomade and makeup on his face were slightly nauseating. They gave him eyebrows that met above his nose. "Go over to the cameras," they said. "For your screen test."

"Don't look at the camera!" they screamed. "Don't look at the lamps!" they screamed.

What the deuce! Where should he look? At the light? It would blind him. The camera? They'd tell him he wasn't *photogénique.*

"Look at the set, choose some unobtrusive tack and push it in!"

(Choosing's all well and good, but how were they going to get him out of here without him dragging the set away, too?)

Action! The little wheels were spinning, the light was hissing, the lights man was on the spot, the boss in the thousand-franc jersey was screaming: "Over there! Over here! *Comme ça!* More! *En face!* Action!"

Phooey! Konoteshenko was nowhere in sight.

Next to Gerasim Gavrilovich—to cut costs—the brigand was twisting and turning his heavily browed mug and following the same commands.

Then they said show up for an answer in three days and

declined any responsibility for removing the makeup from his face. When Gerasim Gavrilovich went home it was three o'clock. The streets were empty, the factory was droning away. The Cabaret was empty. It was the midday break at Boris Gavrilovich's hairdressing salon: a lady was having her hair curled.

Gerasim Gavrilovich thought about how if this turned out to be his star, if he turned out to be *photogénique*, his whole life would start over. He would have plenty of money. He would have his picture taken and pass out cards to his acquaintances. His wife would start enjoying life. He would rub his famous brother Boris Gavrilovich's nose in it. One fine day he might decide to have something tasty to eat or buy himself new trousers. . . . Not everyone was lucky in life, not everyone was *photogénique*. Take Konoteshenko, look at all the people he knew at the *société anonyme*, but he wasn't an actor. If such a fortunate honor were to befall Gerasim Gavrilovich, his fate in this world would not be the hard fate of an infantryman and worker.

He wandered the streets for a long time that day. He decided against going back to the factory: it felt odd for an actor to be going to a factory. He returned home as night was falling. In the courtyard, the Chinese were pouring water over each other, the rich neighbors had their gramophone cranking out a fashionable dance, and his own, Gerasim Gavrilovich's, children were playing noisily up and down the stairs.

Gerasim Gavrilovich washed up, leaving grime on the towel. His wife was hunched over at the kitchen table.

"You and I very definitely have to talk," she said to him in a way that was actually kind. "Do you think you might find a free half-hour? And could you possibly think logically, too?"

He gave her a big smile, asked her to wait another three days, and left the building again.

It was that hour when the lamp is lit over the grocer's, when the delicious smell of cutlets wafts from the bistros' open doors, when, at last, even the indefatigable Boris Gavrilovich closes his doors and locks his shutters—but does not stop working: he lets his regular clients in through the back door. And from the street you catch the faint fragrance of the now hidden salon, a pink light shows through a crack, and if you put your ear to the shutters, you can hear the *tsik-tsik-tsik* of his long, light scissors.

Gerasim Gavrilovich stood there listening to this scissoring, and it grabbed him by the soul, the way brass horns did. It was dark outside, dark, empty, and joyless. He thought about himself, about his nasty and messy life, about the hard times, the foreign climate, and the law of geographical space by the grace of which he had had his rightful soil taken away. The scissors kept up their quiet scissoring behind the shutters, and the air continued to be filled with the smell of dust and perfume.

The three days passed. Gerasim Gavrilovich either lay on the bed or sauntered from street to street. He borrowed money against the future. His wife stopped crying. Their three small children were almost ready to go to school—they were of an age to made literate.

The hour arrived for Gerasim Gavrilovich to return to the *société anonyme*.

Even though it was all under the same high roof as before, it seemed a little stuffier. The brigand was already sitting awaiting sentence. Gerasim Gavrilovich sat down as well. He noticed complicated cameras and preoccupied people walking around who were also enigmas, but the usual lights were still burning.

There was no Konoteshenko to be seen. He began pondering his near future. What kind of rôles would he have to play? Would they be very small? Would he have to depict any disreputable characters? Would they start criticizing him and swearing at him? Would he inadvertently ruin the film with his face and be dragged off to court to pay the costs?

His heart was heavy in anticipation of the appointed hour. Next to him, the brigand was clenching and unclenching his fists and biting his lip; he could not seem to relax. Gerasim Gavrilovich, although in agony, actually surprised himself by feeling sleepy.

After a little while the boss came out.

"You," he said to the brigand, "you can get the hell out of here: we don't need you. But you"—this to Gerasim Gavrilovich—"you really are photogenic. We have no objections to that."

The brigand's eyes reddened, and he stalked off. Gerasim Gavrilovich was left standing in the middle of the studio. Someone came out to take a look at him. The thousand-franc jersey flashed before his eyes.

"Go get made up," they said. "Shooting's in half an hour. We'll show you what to do."

They started applying makeup to Gerasim Gavrilovich, giving him a single eyebrow. This time the kohl wouldn't adhere to him and the makeup man struggled. Konoteshenko came in and shyly watched his friend from the sidelines.

"The die is cast for you," he whispered. "Gerasim Gavrilovich, give it your all! Later they'll take you to Spain, for a hundred francs a day, all expenses paid. The bosses had a discussion about your unusual looks yesterday."

They dressed Gerasim Gavrilovich in tatters and brought him out. He started feeling uneasy. What was all that about a tailcoat, then? he thought.

A señorita came out through hidden doors and dropped her purse. It was a beaded purse, crocheted, the devil knew what was inside it! Gerasim Gavrilovich was rooted to the spot; he couldn't move. And all he had to do was pick up the purse, hide it in his shirt, and retreat into the shadows as if nothing had happened.

"Pick it up!" they shouted at him, "since you're so photogenic. You're just missing one little thing. Heaven sent you what's most important" (or something like that).

Gerasim Gavrilovich stood there staring at the purse. Doubt gripped him, shyness overwhelmed him. The fact that all this had to take place in full view of everyone, and the fact that the purse belonged to someone else—it all embarrassed him.

The jersey repeated the instructions: "Today you happen to have to pick up someone else's purse. A dropped purse, with gold in it. You're also going to have to hide it under your shirt. You've certainly got the right expression on your face for that."

The señorita laughed, and the others laughed, but somebody was getting annoyed.

Gerasim Gavrilovich girded himself. He picked up the purse and went to give it to the jersey. He saw Konoteshenko standing to one side. Konoteshenko was embarrassed.

"The die was cast for you," he said.

They explained it to him a third time and measured out his steps. Again the señorita started walking and dropped her purse.

Gerasim Gavrilovich ran after her, snatched the purse off the ground, and shoved it into her hand. The cameramen actually cursed in French; they could no longer vouch for their patience.

Gerasim Gavrilovich was just not cut out to be an actor.

"Take the makeup off this *photogénique*," they said. "To hell with him!"

The señorita looked at him sympathetically:

"Why not let him try playing the grandee? I like him."

As if he could be a grandee! Gerasim Gavrilovich went to take off his Spanish tatters and scrub the grease from his eyebrows. He thought about looking for Konoteshenko before he left, but his friend had made himself scarce.

No one watched him go, no one looked round. So he quit those parts and went home, having failed to fall in step with the times. He left sanguinely and bought the French evening paper on his way—to read the classifieds again. He recalled certain past victories on the front of daily life, though they were very far in the past, nothing worth going into.

That day, I ran into him as night was falling.

"So, Gerasim Gavrilovich, how are things? How is your personal relationship with Monsieur Renault?"

"Broken."

"How's your health in general and in particular?"

"My eyes have been hurting for days. The daylight bothers them."

"Why is that?"

Then he told me the whole story.

"So," he said, "Grisha, have you ever heard anything like it? Or maybe read it in the papers?"

I thought for a moment. I said:

"Never heard it or read it. Nowadays the papers prefer to write about the opposite, about jutting chins and people getting ahead. I'm afraid no one's going to want to read about you."

I felt no regret whatsoever at that moment. We left our regret and our baggage back in Sevastopol.

1929

The Argentine

Kind sirs, gentle ladies, my apologies! Particularly to the ladies, for not everything in my tale will be equally high-minded. Ivan Pavlovich has suffered a real fiasco. That is exactly what he said as he was leaving: "Grisha, my friend, this has been a real fiasco with you in Paris." There was nothing I could say to that. It was frankly embarrassing because the fiasco was in part my fault. As the train pulled out I waved my handkerchief, the way we do here.

Ivan Pavlovich arrived from the provinces the Friday before last, leaving his rabbit farm in the hands of his partner, K. P. Birilev, seaman and rabbit farmer. Ivan Pavlovich had been writing to me for a whole year about how he could not get along without a female of Russian origin anymore and that, come what may, he had resolved to marry. "Grisha, my friend," he wrote, "will you understand me? You're young, you're living in the capital of the arts, you have charming ladies at your beck and call, you might say, by virtue of your fortunate appearance. Whereas I—it's not enough that I carry the sad burden of my forty-five years of age and a shortage of hair, but I'm also mired in breeding these rabbits here, far from any entertainments. Our farm is desolate, the house is dirty and uncomfortable, the suits Konstantin Birilev and I have to wear at times go unmended. It's a crying shame. When it comes to our borscht, it's harder for us than someone else in the fields. . . . Grisha, find me a Russian bride, someone who won't look down on our rural quiet, who can be housewifely and not too exacting when it comes to male beauty. Remember that Konstantin Birilev is younger than me and slimmer. My dear Grisha, understand that I am your only uncle and that you have no other relatives in the world."

Letters like this arrived no less than once a month, and each time they gave my heart a good stab. The pictures he drew of rural life were not reassuring. But what was I to do? Ivan Pavlovich had erred in many points on my happy account: I don't live in a world center, I live next door, in Billancourt; I kill myself in the factory from morning til night; I don't know many young ladies, and those I do all have their caps set on handsome positions (like waiting on tables at the *Rose des Alpes*), and I'd be disgracing myself if I suggested they travel three hours from Paris to cook borscht, even for love. And as far as mending suits goes, I would feel awkward even bringing it up.

Nonetheless, about three months ago, one rainy May evening, when a sudden sadness and forlornness came over me and I felt like a friendly gaze, I went to see Madame Klava at the Hotel Caprice and laid it all out for her.

Madame Klava covered her naked mannequin with a towel, asked me for a cigarette, and fell to thinking.

"Maybe," she said, cocking her pretty head, "maybe your uncle would be satisfied with a hired worker. Nothing could be easier than that. For instance, I have one acquaintance, he's out of a job right now, I could recommend him because if you're going to hire someone, then of course it should be a man."

Our ill-fated conversation ended abruptly at that. In parting, I kissed Klava's pretty hand.

But one day Madame Klava greeted me at the grocer's, took me by the sleeve, and asked me to betake myself to the Cabaret for an urgent and confidential chat.

The news Klava had to report was fateful for Ivan Pavlovich: a family of workers had arrived in Paris from Estonia, and through the efforts of our committees they were going to be sent either to the south of France, to do agricultural work, or else to Canada. This party was being housed for the time being near one of the city gates. Among the arrivals was an acquaintance of Klava's, a certain Selindrin, and with him, in addition to his lawful wife and three children, there was also his sister, an unmarried girl of nineteen by the name of Antonina Nikolaevna Selindrina.

That very same evening I wrote a letter to Ivan Pavlovich demanding his presence. I reported the young woman's name and age and the quickest route to my place from the train station, and when I came home from the factory that Friday, Ivan Pavlovich was sitting by the window in my tiny room waiting for me. He immediately reported that he had seen the top of the Eiffel Tower when he was crossing the bridge. In the two years of our bitter separation he had picked up more color and looked healthier, but his eyes still burned. In his bundle, by the way, he had brought some eggs and a marvelous rabbit pâté. There was no end to our merriment that evening.

In the morning, when I woke up in bed next to Ivan Pavlovich, I confess I started examining him from Antonina Nikolaevna Selindrina's perspective, and I must admit—I liked what I saw. His beard was black and of magnificent proportions, you might say. His big nose, a little crooked but mighty of form, showed equally his strength of character and his great heartfelt gentleness. Ivan Pavlovich's teeth (his mouth was slightly open) were strong and yellow and lent a manly expression to his sleeping face. In short, I giddily imagined Ivan Pavlovich, a flower in his buttonhole, standing on the steps of Billancourt City Hall arm in arm with Antonina Selindrina. . . . The factory whistle drove me out of the building.

It was decided to go make Antonina Nikolaevna's acquaintance on Sunday afternoon. I won't elaborate on our Saturday evening. Ivan Pavlovich didn't say or eat very much, but he did sigh often and deeply, especially at Boris Gavrilovich the hairdresser's, where we both went after we'd had a bite, and where it was after eight before they were done with us (the usual Saturday story!). But afterward we smelled good enough for the entire Rue Nationale, like real suitors!

Sunday morning, Ivan Pavlovich attended mass. At half past one in the afternoon, in the even July weather, we emerged from the building in elevated spirits and headed into the city. We had at least half an hour's trolley ride to the city gate where the Estonian party of refugees had been camped out since the previous week. Now Ivan Pavlovich initiated a conversation with me that had evidently been weighing on him ever since his arrival.

"Grisha," he said to me, "What do you think, can I be a woman's happiness?"

Without stopping to think I answered yes.

"Grisha," he went on. "Tell me before God whether there isn't something repulsive about my appearance. Or suspect in my fate. Or comical about my behavior."

Seeing how terribly upset he was about his impending happiness, I began consoling him with all my heart.

"Ivan Pavlovich," I said as firmly as possible. "You are a
superb man, as far as I know you, and if you only take a liking
to Mademoiselle Selindrina, then of course you'll make her
happy by linking your fates. Just think: you're set up, you're a
landowner in a certain sense, your business is going great guns.
You're taking for your wife an unmarried girl who has nothing,
an orphan who is a burden to her family, an unmarried girl who
in all likelihood is being exploited by her brother and his
wife—the way I have been exploited, for example, by Monsieur
Renault. You'll marry her, she'll acquire a protector in life and
become the mistress of your holdings. What does she have to
look forward to without you? Russian refugees from the
Estonian land, hard work somewhere in Australia or Canada.
And you can be her bulwark for her whole life if only she suits
your fancy."

"My fancy!" exclaimed Ivan Pavlovich with a bitter chuck-
le. "Grisha, you're a lucky man if you don't know what it means
to live without a woman, without a wife, when there's no one
chirping around you, when your house is empty, orphaned.
When you have no one to open up to."

I thought about Madame Klava and held my tongue.

We got off the trolley at the right stop and began walking
toward the Porte d'Italie.

Ivan Pavlovich didn't walk, though, he flew, and I flew in
his wake. His hat could not have looked better on him; his navy
suit, his light-colored tie and beetle tiepin, his brand-new
brown shoes, everything was first-rate. For all his chic, though,
even from far away you would never have taken Ivan Pavlovich

for some unprincipled dandy or loose-living fashion plate. No, both his figure and his face expressed profound contemplation, a mind focused on a single object. Near the gate they pointed out a long wooden barracks to us. We entered the yard.

It goes without saying that we found squalor and poverty and a lack of French here in abundance. The cries—to say nothing of the smells—of children hung in the air. Evidently life in the barracks differs in no way from life in the freight cars during the revolution—the same filth and overcrowding, the men quartered separately from the women. On the women's side they were doing laundry, cooking, smacking howling children. . . . In short, there was plenty to gawk at.

The first person we saw was a tall, black-haired young woman wearing black stockings, laced boots, and a black scarf. We asked her if she couldn't find Antonina Nikolaevna Selindrina for us.

"That is I," she said, and she bowed.

"Ah," I thought, "the other four aren't here to watch! What a pleasant surprise."

Ivan Pavlovich tipped his hat.

"Allow me to introduce myself," he said, not without gravity. "Kudrin, Ivan Pavlovich Kudrin. And this is my friend and nephew, Grisha."

Antonina Nikolaevna bowed again. She wore her hair parted in the middle, her dark eyebrows spread in arcs across her brow, and under them her eyes watched us, a little apprehensive but pleasant nonetheless. She did not smile.

"I think you were forewarned about our visit?" I asked, hinting at Madame Klava. "Could we go to the nearby café and drink a little tea?"

"No," she said, and she shook her head. "I really mustn't leave. The children are coming down with something and they might call for me."

So the three of us remained in the middle of this unseemly yard to talk.

"I've heard, Antonina Nikolaevna, that you and your family are planning to go to Canada," said Ivan Pavlovich rather animatedly. "Doesn't such a long journey frighten you? True, now some daredevils fly across the ocean in a day, but isn't it about eight days' voyage by ship?"

She looked at Ivan Pavlovich mournfully.

"No, I'm not afraid," she said. "If it's eight, then it's eight."

"Weren't you sorry to leave your native land?"

A spark flashed in her eyes.

"No, I didn't mind."

"No doubt exotic, faraway places must beckon you?"

"What are you saying?"

"I'm saying that foreign lands might also be to your taste. In Estonia, I'm saying, there aren't so many fish in the sea."

"Yes, certainly."

"Only, you see, there you have to work so very hard, and we know what America's like. They say it's nothing but desperate Fordization everywhere."

"I'm not afraid of work."

"Well, naturally, especially if you're traveling with your family, together, it means there'll be work."

She blushed suddenly and her lips trembled. I tugged at Ivan Pavlovich's sleeve.

"And how do you like France? Paris, for example? Or (what Paris!) the French provinces?"

"I haven't seen Paris," she said with an effort. "I haven't had any time to take in the sights. The children are coming down with something. When I was at the *gymnasium* . . ."

She drew her scarf across her chest and fell silent.

"Antonina Nikolaevna," Ivan Pavlovich said suddenly. "Has anyone told you anything about me?"

"Yes, Klavdia Sergeevna," said Antonina Nikolaevna with relief. "She said you're looking for . . ."

"A helper!" exclaimed Ivan Pavlovich, overjoyed. "You see, I have a small farm, that is, Konstantin Birilev and I have a farm: rabbits, such stupid animals, I'll tell you, but they do keep multiplying. . . . And you know it's hard for us alone, it's hard on a farm, and—forgive me—sad. Our work's not hard and there's plenty to eat. And we would divide up all our income three ways."

"Good luck!" I thought, and I moved off to the side.

Antonina Nikolaevna stood silent and her brows knitted together slightly.

"I am forty-five years old," continued Ivan Pavlovich, more measuredly now. "We only started this business two years ago, but it's not going badly, you can ask around, the business is going extremely well. I'm not a mean man, my God, just ask Grisha. What's there to say, you still have time to get to know me, but I already know you now: as soon as I saw you, I knew. I beg of you, Antonina Nikolaevna, be my wife."

An honest man might not have looked at her at that moment. I did. I saw her long black skirt above her perfectly decent but sturdy shoes, her shoulders wrapped in the old scarf. The sleeves of her blouse were too short, her slender hands with black cracks on her fingers stuck out, so she hid them under her scarf.

He blurted this out with stunning directness and took a step toward Antonina Nikolaevna. She paled noticeably.

"I thank you," she whispered so softly I could barely hear her. "But I cannot be your wife."

Ivan Pavlovich stopped, rooted to the ground.

"Why is that? Am I so repulsive?" he asked, frightened.

Antonina Nikolaevna shook her head. Tears glistened under her fluttering eyelashes.

"There's been some misunderstanding," she whispered. "I thought you came to hire me as a worker."

Ivan Pavlovich didn't budge. He dropped his head and looked at the dusty, stone-paved yard.

"It's an insult if you don't explain," uttered Ivan Pavlovich hesitantly. "As an honest man and soldier, I beg of you. . . . Grisha my friend, move back a little more."

She turned white, her eyes darted, and her lips pursed.

"I cannot insult you. Forgive me. They got me drunk, they tricked me . . . I'm in my third month."

There was a long moment of silence.

"There's been some misunderstanding," repeated Antonina Nikolaevna, "and I beg of you not to say anything to Klavdia Sergeevna. No one knows about this except my sister-in-law and my brother. I thought you'd come to hire me as a worker."

I couldn't see his face, he had his back to me, but I was amazed he was still standing. Then Antonina Nikolaevna's face changed, and she fiddled with the scarf on her chest.

Finally a shudder ran through Ivan Pavlovich's entire body and he regained his senses.

"So that's how it is," he uttered slowly. "A misunderstanding. No, I don't need a worker. I apologize for the disturbance."

He turned around and walked toward the gate, and I started after him. When we reached the street I couldn't restrain myself and looked back: Selindrina was standing there watching us walk away.

"Got her drunk and tricked her," repeated Ivan Pavlovich to himself. "And what was her brother doing at the time? But she didn't stay in Estonia—that means she had nowhere to go. Grisha, there's a case for you. Right? There is real shame!"

I didn't dare look at him.

"I'm the one to blame for it all, Ivan Pavlovich, my idiotic carelessness has wrecked everything. I summoned you to Paris, made you waste your money, like an idiot took you to the barber's yesterday. But I'm not going to leave it like this with Madame Klava."

My anger flared out of all proportion at that moment.

"Quiet, Grisha," said Ivan Pavlovich. "I gave her my word not to tell anyone, and don't you dare. After all, it's her disgrace. Can you imagine what she's putting up with from her sister-in-law?"

And he suddenly blushed in the strongest possible way.

Fury was raging through me, and I didn't know how to calm myself. I felt guilty before Ivan Pavlovich, and I was ashamed to look him in the eye. All Klava's old offenses came to mind there in the trolley. Antonina weighed on my imagination as well. When we got home, Ivan Pavlovich sat by the window in his underwear.

"Tomorrow I'll be leaving you, Grisha," he said. "There's nothing more for me to do here. I've made a fool of myself, and it's time I went back. But who could wreck her life that way? Maybe the *gymnasium* teacher? Or was it just some harmonica-playing pig from the factory?"

Tears of admiration sprung from my eyes at these words. "If only he'd curse me, if only he'd get angry and berate me!" I prayed. "If only he'd put Antonina in her proper place."

"Let it pass, Ivan Pavlovich. If you want to contemplate every fallen woman you come across, you're just wasting your time."

He turned red again and sat bolt upright.

"Are you out of your mind? You think she's fallen? You understand nothing about women, brother."

I ate without appetite that day and did not return until late, but Ivan Pavlovich was already asleep. Early in the morning we said goodbye, but when I returned in the evening he was still here, sitting on my chair. He hadn't gone anywhere that day.

"Forgive me, Grisha," he said, embarrassed. "I'll leave you tomorrow. For today I'll have to crowd you a little longer."

Then I saw a change come over him that was not like this sturdy man: his thoughts were in total disarray. At dinner he asked for some vodka with his Cossack cutlets, and that night he got up several times (he slept on the outside) and muttered to himself.

Tuesday morning we said goodbye once more. In parting he said: "What do you think, Grisha, under American laws, will she have a hard time of it, with the child and all?"

I didn't know American laws any more than he did, and he obviously was not expecting me to answer.

"No, tell me this instead: Does her sister-in-law rag her from morning til night? She does rag her, doesn't she?"

"Almost certainly."

And again he didn't leave. What can I say! He stayed with me all the way until Thursday, when a postcard arrived from K. P. Birilev urgently requesting his return.

When I came home Thursday evening (en route I encountered but pretended not to recognize Klava, though why was she to blame? After all, according to *her*, she didn't know anything about it), and when I walked into my room and saw Ivan Pavlovich in his navy suit with the beetle I guessed he had made up his mind. In the past week, the city atmosphere in my room and the lack of healthy movement had robbed him of some of his robust country color. But there was new energy in his eyes, and I remembered his yellow teeth, which I'd once seen—a mark of great courage.

"Grisha, take me there," he told me simply. "I won't be able to find the way by myself. Let her give birth, I'll adopt the child, I'll leave him the rabbits when I die. I can't let this go, all these days I've been in agony, body and soul. Let her move in with me, let her live there for the time being—and then we'll see. She did have very wonderful eyes. And such skinny shoulders, did you notice? And remember her pretty scarf? True, no one wears those scarves anymore, of course."

"I remember the eyes, and the shoulders, and the pretty scarf," I thought at that moment, "but still I never expected this."

But Ivan Pavlovich didn't give me a chance to regain my senses. In his delight he kept pestering me so that five minutes later, without even changing clothes or washing up, I found myself on my way to Paris. He was walking beside me in happy contemplation, and I . . . God knows what didn't cross my mind in those moments! Thoughts were flying at me like doves, and my soul was hovering in the sky. The light was fading. The haze of the hot day hung over the buildings. Ivan Pavlovich and I were walking to the edge of the world, and I kept looking at him, shocked and pleased.

This was our mood as we rode the trolley as well, mostly in silence, so that people might have assumed each of us was riding separately, and, indeed, given the difference in our suits, there was no way they would connect us. And this, too, cheered me up.

So we're walking up to the gate and we see the barracks. It's evening. It's dusty. Men are carting in beer. The posters on the fences have changed since we were here, a new drama has been pasted up. We walk up to the barracks and enter the yard. It's quiet. The windows and doors are locked. Ivan Pavlovich is terrified.

"Let's go to that bistro nearby, Grisha," he says. "We'll ask the owner what changes there have been in our absence."

We go to the bistro. "They left," the husband and wife who own the bistro tell us. "The day before yesterday they were all taken away to Argentina, to the plantations."

(Through the attentions of our committees, that means.)

We ask, "Maybe they didn't all go, maybe not absolutely everyone, so to speak? Maybe someone stayed, guessing he would not find happiness in Argentina?"

They answer: "No, no one guessed anything, we haven't heard anything like that."

"Grisha, what's going on? How am I supposed to understand this?" exclaimed Ivan Pavlovich. But he exclaimed this on Friday, the next day. On Thursday, he had said nothing to me or the bistro owners. He walked out and saw the men carting the beer again. . . .

Isn't it in Argentina that everyone dances the tango?

1929

About the Hooks

Madame Klava said to me:

"Why is it, Grishenka, you're always writing about people you know, about such ordinary and, to be perfectly frank, boring people? One fails at a career in the cinema, another loses out on a bride, and I can't even remember what the third one did. They're all such colorless characters, really! Write us a few words about a king of nature, some American type who sets your heart to pounding so hard you want to drop everything and run after him to snatch a moment of insane happiness, move in with the man and spin a beautiful fairy tale together."

"I don't have an American type," I replied. "Where am I going to get an American type? There was one gentleman, though, a man, not a boy, who came close to being like that. About as close as I am to you."

"Well, then? If it didn't work out for him, you can invent an ending to make it more intriguing."

"My name would be mud. Everyone figured out a long time ago there weren't any American types on my horizon."

She lapsed into thought.

"All right, then write it down just the way it was and then we'll see. Write the whole truth and leave in his real first name and patronymic and his real last name, too."

Fine. I got home, sat down at my desk, and wrote a story about Alexander Evgrafovich Barabanov. There is such a person, and there was a time when he and I had occasion to see quite a lot of one another.

I began my story with a description of the weather. Lots of Russian writers don't sneer at the weather. In fact, for some that's their only claim to fame. Our writers can pay more attention to nature because their material situation is better than others'. And if someone has no material concerns, who are you to say where he should look at nature? The weather there is closer and more obvious. It can soak you to your very bones, soak you all the way to your soul, especially if there's a little rain.

It was a cold, rainy, windy, raw, tedious autumn day—that's how I began. There wasn't any sky at all this time, I mean, undoubtedly there was somewhere very high up, near the other planets, for instance, or very far away, say, in Orel or Kazan. In Paris, though, there wasn't any sky, there were clouds. They raced thickly above our reckless heads and from time to time crossed our field of vision. We had lots of clouds, more than we needed. And God only knows how forlorn it felt.

Alexander Evgrafovich Barabanov walked out of the train station onto the square, and his heart started pounding, who knows why. It was probably a little of everything—hope, loneliness, presentiment, penury, and anything but first youth, all of it strung lightly together, which is why his heart started pounding. Alexander Evgrafovich stopped for a moment by the station exit; he looked as if he were saying a quick prayer. In fact, he had had a perfectly useless, unconscionably stupid idea: What if this raw autumn wind, which is so bad for rheumatics, were to pull me from this very Parisian train station, right back across the threshold, and onto a train, and it took me down all my old roads, through Thionville (where he had just come from), through Liège, Uzhgorod, Belgrade, Alexandria, the Princes Islands, on ships, trains, roads, and rivers? And what if I were to wind up with fleas on the lower deck of an English steamer and we were to dock, the last stage in our journeying, on Odessa's shores (which is where it all began)? This whole appalling idea flashed through Barabanov's mind and vanished just as quickly. And Alexander Evgrafovich moved off not in the reverse direction but forward. How is it, speaking in general now, that a man's legs can hold him up?

He walked down the stairs, marveled at the number of newspapers in the kiosk, and noticed the flower store on the left-hand side as you go toward the trolley stop. Trolleys kept passing him without explanation. Then he stuck his hands in his pockets.

His left hand was holding his left pocket, where something had stirred for a moment; his right hand felt for his wallet, and he recited the familiar address by heart, only now it seemed different and fresh, not like when he had read it before. Before he'd read it platonically: here's the street and the address, and here's the trolley he's supposed to take. Now he was face to face with that trolley and in a little while he'd come face to face with the street and house and . . .

The trolley carrying Alexander Evgrafovich set out with a whistle, a bell, and a rumble.

What a city Paris is! A new arrival is the least of its concerns! You could be a Solomon and people would still rush past and not one of them would look round. You might feel like embracing the whole world, but no one cares in the least. You might, like a certain famous boy, have your vitals gnawed upon by a fox. Well, you can have your fox because no one cares. It's not, as I say, like in Orel or Kazan. And in this regard, our new arrivals divide up into two neat categories: some tell themselves (I remember, I was like this), That's fine, if you don't want to then I won't look at you either, to hell with you, even if you are handsome and famous and damn magnificent. And it's true—provided they don't look for an hour or two after their journey, or if they keep themselves in check until dusk, if they exercise restraint. Others, accustomed from their travels to every kind of humiliation, sear it with their gaze. We don't care if Paris grinds us in the mud by ignoring us, what we're doing is small, what we're doing is admiring the capital of the world if ever we have the chance—just wait—to visit it while passing through. Paris, not Tristan d'Acuna.

Alexander Evgrafovich not only admired Paris, his gaze seared everything, from the signs on the buildings to the nail on the conductor's pinky. He sympathetically weighed each exquisite detail of the city, each blemish on its face. When he got off the trolley, he inquired about the rest of his way and proceeded on foot, standing for a long time at a certain intersection (we know which one), admiring the elevated train, which rested on stone piers in the middle of the street. And peculiar thoughts ran through his mind. Commercial thoughts.

He arrived at the address—a large and prosperous apartment building. The concierge's wife showed him to the elevator and pressed the button. The narrow doors slammed shut on his nose and fingers several times. "Oh my, the doors here bite," he thought. As he got out, they struck him in the neck again. He sent the contraption back down and stood on the landing for a moment. And new thoughts again crept into his mind. And again, they were commercial.

He walked in, still holding on to his left pocket, where something had been wriggling around for a long time, but was now quiet. He was asked to wait. He sat down with dignity and asked for a glass of water. They brought him water, he took a ceremonious sip and handed the glass back. He was trying to hear who was talking in the next room. Who exactly? Wasn't that the voice of a fourteen-year-old girl? (Yes, a full fourteen years already, just see how time flies!) Wasn't that little Liubochka's voice he heard?

A fine gentleman walked in. He was a businessman, a man who had seen to his own best interests, a high-flying bird from the looks of him, with very very clean hands, clean-shaven, impeccable, who looked as if he were part of this magnificent city, as if he'd been born here and had never left.

"Hello, Pavel Petrovich," said Alexander Evgrafovich, standing at attention.

"Hello. Here you have Barabanov."

Pavel Petrovich reached out with both hands and touched Alexander Evgrafovich on the shoulders.

"Ah! Barabanov! Very pleased. So pleased. Very, very pleased. We've been looking forward to seeing you."

Both men sat down at the desk. There was a tremendous quantity of papers on it, as well as a telephone, and a Russian abacus, and a typewriter—no, I'm lying! two typewriters. And next to the inkwell, a single flower in a glass.

Alexander Evgrafovich inquired respectfully:

"Have you been well, Pavel Petrovich? What about Maria Danilovna? And your mama?"

"Everyone's fine and dandy, we're doing fine, no one's starving. What about you?"

"We're fine, thank God. And Liubochka?"

"Liubochka, too. . . . We've been considering your proposal. It's an interesting idea."

"Since I didn't receive an answer to my letter and thought I might speed things up, I decided to make the first move, Pavel Petrovich. I arrived this morning from the provinces especially to talk things over with you. And here, I brought Liubochka . . . "

"This morning? And straight to see me? Very energetic on your part. Let's talk."

"Here, I brought Liubochka . . ."

"Liubochka is well, too, *merci*. Studying, the top student at her school, a great girl. So then, let's think this through, the what and how of it, and together we'll earn a crust of bread and butter."

Barabanov focused his thoughts, wiggled his fingers, and became very still.

"Personally, Pavel Petrovich, I don't need a commission, just whatever you think is right. Instead of a commission I'd like you to arrange for a certain patent."

"An invention of yours?"

"Yes. You know all the ins and outs, you know how to see any kind of business through. Instead of a commission I'd like the patent on my invention and let that settle my fate."

"Fine, that's what we'll do. It's not hard. You mean you've gone and become a real businessman?"

"Of course not! That's easier said than done. This all comes from too much spare time. Your mind is constantly working, it's exhausting, your head hurts. Even now, on my way to see you, I had the glimmer of an idea about using the free space between the piers under the train tracks. For instance, you could get a concession from the municipal administration to put in a garage there, or a bathhouse, or a shop. The space is going to waste, despite all the modern overcrowding! Or take those little elevator doors: it's a flawed mechanism!"

"Easy now, easy!" exclaimed Pavel Petrovich. "To begin with, tell me everything you know about that, about the first business, about what you wrote. About the hooks."

Barabanov placed one foot next to the other.

"As I wrote you, Pavel Petrovich, we were taking down the military wire in what was once a front zone. Well, we worked for a month, we worked for two, we actually got used to the wire, we couldn't have asked for anything better even. Then they switched us to clearing bombshells—all under the same contract. Well, we made our peace with that, too. I wouldn't say we came to love the bombshells like our own children, of course, but we didn't complain, and then about a month ago I had a commercial idea, but whom was I to share it with? Only you might know how to see this kind of thing through."

"Well, then, go on."

"Here was my idea: Even the most miserable spent bombshell has a small copper hook on its side which has its own independent value, as a metal, naturally. That's when it occurred to me: find some clever person in the big wide world with capital—you, for instance, Pavel Petrovich Gutenshtam—and let him buy up all these hooks, melt them down (giving our shop the job, by the way), and sell the metal by weight. If you melted it down properly, you might get half a million in copper. I'd also like to arrange for a patent for an idea of mine."

"Who do you think you'd be dealing with?"

"I've thought everything through, everything, it's kind of funny actually. First I wondered whether it might not be some kind of illegal act here. I started asking my boss questions: Doesn't someone need those hooks? No, it wouldn't be so hard to do, they told me. The minister would authorize a concession, they said, the governor is moaning and groaning about what to do with those hooks, they said. The authorities would certainly give their approval once they knew you intended to see the business through."

"Who does that depend on, the military ministry or the civil authorities?"

"The military, exactly. You get a contract from them, for knocking off the hooks. The hooks, you see, will pay for it. You hire a shop—we have about thirty of our men there, and also Andrei Nikanorych, remember him from Rostov? This year a priest came for the Feast of the Dormition and conducted a service, and we subscribe to two newspapers. This is a job for them. You keep the records, and you don't have to ship the hooks anywhere because right next door, in Metz, there's a plant that casts steel. It's prepared to buy up all your copper and is also interested in my little patent. I've already made inquiries."

"Do you know people there?"

"Yes. Among the lower classes, but useful ones, they might come in handy."

Pavel Petrovich pursed his lips and pulled at his nose.

"How much money do you want?"

Barabanov became flustered.

"I just need to cover my travel expenses, I'm not interested in any bonuses. My patent will settle my fate. I hope my patent won't be too much trouble for you?"

"Not at all. But first let's get this hook business settled. Today I'll call one extremely influential person, get some information from him, then I'll go see someone else, also a very interesting person—with the necessary pull. After these two conversations, I'll calculate what our profit might be. Come by tomorrow at the same time and bring your passport and patent. If my calculations are favorable we'll send your papers off to a special department right away. I'll pay you half a percent of the gross on the hooks, so if the deal is worth half a million, you'll get two and a half thousand. We'll do the math, send in the patent, and tomorrow evening we'll go to the site so that I can get familiar with the situation."

Alexander Evgrafovich stood up:

"I hope we can see this through."

Pavel Petrovich stood up as well. His ears were burning, shot through with a pinkish light, like apricots. He made a dry sound rubbing his hands together, adjusted his pince-nez, and smoothed his eyebrow.

"Mmm, yes."

"I'll be going now, Pavel Petrovich. Please say hello to Maria Danilovna and your mama."

"Thank you, I certainly will. Until tomorrow then?"

"And Liubochka. I brought her this . . ."

"And Liubochka, certainly. She's at school right now, classes started last week. They work so hard."

"I have here . . ."

"Certainly. I'll tell her everything. She remembers you and

once asked me, 'What ever happened to Barabanov, Papochka? Such a smart man, really.'"

"Say hello for me."

He retreated, and retreated some more, toward the doors, the first set, then the second. The new and improved lock clicked. One more step and he found himself on the staircase and the door shut behind him. All of a sudden it was very quiet. Then a truck drove by, the building shook and settled down. A ragman cried out in the courtyard.

Alexander Evgrafovich pressed his hand to his left pocket. He took a cautious step away from the door and started taking out something that was trying to leap out of his hands. In his palm he held a lop-eared puppy of indeterminate breed with paws curled under and a limp tail. During their conversation Barabanov had not found a way to give it to Pavel Petrovich for Liubochka. Sometimes Barabanov lost all his resolve over the small things.

He went downstairs, stowing the puppy in his pocket, and walked down the street. What a city this was! What a city— don't take this for undue enthusiasm—Paris was! The gray day was blustery, the sky was lowering onto your head, the noise rent your soul, and roasted chestnuts tempted you from the street corners.

Barabanov was in no rush. He seemed as confident of himself as he would have been of the most loyal friend. It never occurred to him to find refuge in some Hotel Caprice. He had exactly twenty-three francs and change, and another ten he'd borrowed, and, naturally, his return ticket to his place of residence. But until tomorrow, until his final departure, there was nothing more he needed.

He walked without a thought to where he was going. He surveyed all kinds of different streets, long and short, commercial and seigniorial, and saw a tower above the buildings a few times, but had no way of reaching that tower, which kept receding first to his right and then his left. It was better that way. Had he reached the tower, Alexander Evgrafovich would certainly have climbed it with all his commercial ideas and probably would have started thinking up all sorts of nonsense, such as, What if you projected advertising against the tower in the evenings? He started walking through a large formal fall garden, taking an interest in everything, including whether or not they locked the garden at night. Nature's withering was in full swing here: the fountains weren't running, and rotted russet leaves were tossing in the wind, sticking to his shoes, to children's noses, to the umbrellas of the *bonnes* and nannies, who had opened them just in case.

At exactly seven o'clock, Alexander Evgrafovich went to a cafeteria to eat supper, spent fourteen francs plus a tip, and when he was outside fed his left pocket some squished bread. The puppy looked barely alive.

The formal garden was closed. It was quickly growing dark, the gray air was thickening, and streetlamps punched holes in it here and there. Time stretched out down the boulevard with its benches. He sat down and concentrated. He lit a cigarette.

The coming day did not worry him, his outlook was clear as far as the near future was concerned. He had only to recall the satisfied look on Pavel Petrovich Gutenshtam's face in order to await the coming day with equanimity. The military ministry, the factory in Metz, Pavel Petrovich's apartment, the train Barabanov had taken to Paris and would take home tomorrow, all this began reeling by slowly, then faster and faster, in his mind.

The streetlamps suddenly ran at him in rows, they ran fast, but the they couldn't catch up with one another, they ran like strung beads, like copper beads, like round hooks scattered from black space. He couldn't count them all, ninety-nine and a half slipped past him, one last half got caught somewhere close by. This little half was his property. Hundreds of thousands of hooks were flying, and Pavel Petrovich had said—in the pleasant voice of a well-groomed man from the capital—that . . .

"You can't sleep here," a policeman said and walked on.

The boulevard's streetlamps were standing still now, but then the trolley flew by, rumbling over every switch.

Barabanov crossed his left leg over his right, but the puppy in his pocket gave a shrill yelp. He took the little mutt out into the fresh air. This sobered him up. He had spoken of Liubochika a little, mentioned Andrei Nikanorych, vaguely promised something for her tomorrow.

He hadn't had a moment to give Liubochka her present. The whole time he'd been preoccupied with the idea of isolating high-tension currents.

Who on earth cared about high-tension currents? Damned if he knew! Barabanov's invention was devoted to isolating these currents, and his patent concerned this secret. It would settle his destiny, the destiny of a former military man, and the crucial paper was in his pocket, along with Gutenshtam's address, his return ticket, and this year's purple passport. It was all there together on his broad Barabanov chest.

Ahead lay independence. Go where you like, my soul, come and go, make new discoveries!

He turned his collar up. It was nighttime quiet on the boulevard now. He decided the puppy had had enough and put him back in his pocket. His thoughts returned to Pavel Petrovich's desk, and from it—to Liubochka.

She was sleeping sweetly now, the ink washed from her fingers. Her alarm would wake her in the morning, she'd jump up and start running around the room, in a hurry to get to school. She'd put on a dress and fasten her metal beads, but the thread would break and the copper beads would spill down her arms and dress. He had to count them. "Papa, what ever happened to your Barabanov?" shouted Liubochka. "Remember how he used to bounce me on his knee when I was little, in Alexandria?" And the beads were still spilling down with a jingle. Don't miss that one little half, it's yours!

"You can't sleep," the policeman said again, touching him on the shoulder and walking on.

"*Pardon!*" exclaimed Barabanov, and he stood up and walked away.

It was growing light. There, above the rooftops, above the formal garden which God only knew when they'd open, the clouds were growing light and an unexpected rain was falling rapidly on the buildings, the pavement, Barabanov. The shower ended, and the sun rose behind the clouds, not here, but somewhere very high up, near the other planets, or very far away, say in Orel or Kazan. Barabanov was walking through the city, he looked well slept, he looked as if his mood couldn't be better.

He reached Mr. Gutenshtam's apartment at eleven o'clock in the morning. That was his appointment. He had drunk his coffee and eaten four croissants, two eggs, and a sausage sandwich, washed his hands under the spigot at the intersection (you know which one) and splashed a little water on his face. He had had to leave the puppy beside the municipal trash bin: it was unclear what it had died from, whether it had suffocated in Barabanov's pocket or he had crushed it in the night when he fell asleep on the bench. Or whether it had been taken away from its mother too soon. He rang the doorbell. Someone ran to open it. And the ragman cried out from the courtyard below.

He was left standing on the landing. The telephone rang, but no one answered it. He rang the doorbell again. Even if there were five rooms in the apartment, or seven, wouldn't someone hear him ringing? No, there they were, hurrying from far away and exclaiming: "It must be from the office!" And they let him in.

Silence again. Something odd was happening behind the closed doors, some movement. Someone seemed to want to come out to see him in the entry but didn't. The door opened slowly, and Maria Danilovna came out, still holding on to it— her eyes, puffy and her hair uncombed. She who always wore a corset and her hair and hairpieces piled high on her head.

She stopped and stood stock-still. The light had gone out in her eyes, and her red, swollen face started to quiver.

"Barabanov. He had an appointment with you," she said, and she swayed from side to side, this large, heavy woman. "Barabanov, so this is how we meet again. . . . He died, in the night, in his sleep, a heart attack. He went to bed and never woke up. . . ." She was crying, her legs were starting to buckle. Barabanov stood there mute.

"No one dreamed he had a bad heart. Remember how he used to run around and play tennis and all of that? He was out yesterday making inquiries for you. Other men live to be a hundred. When he came back last evening he was so pleased. . . ."

Barabanov said: "I'll leave, I won't keep you. You don't have time for me."

She didn't answer, she was crying. And he walked toward the door. For the briefest of moments he hesitated in front of her. Should he turn around and inquire about Pavel Petrovich's mama, about Liubochka? Or should he leave without saying anything? Or might Liubochka run out of the back rooms at any moment? No one did, though, so he decided to leave. He turned his head as if he were making a low bow; at decisive moments he didn't always know how he should behave.

All of a sudden he remembered the hooks, the night on the boulevard, his dreams, and the fact that sleeping was, in point of fact, forbidden.

And that's the end of my story. I'm afraid it was a little long, especially since Barabanov wasn't from Billancourt, so there's nothing inherently interesting about him for my readers. I'm also afraid people will say that finding the American angle is this story is quite a stretch, like night and day! About as American an angle as Orel or Kazan!

But we've never come across anything closer.

1929

An Incident with Music

Ivan Ivanovich Kondurin was coming home at the usual time. At a quarter to eight, if you must know. His wife, Alexandra Pavlovna, was cooking; two plates, two forks, two knives, the salt shaker, and the bread were on the table. Ivan Ivanovich sat down on a chair and continued thinking.

"What are you doing in there?" his wife shouted from the kitchen. Any kind of silence unsettled this woman.

Ivan Ivanovich scrutinized his hands. Ivan Ivanovich had once been a musician.

In his youth, actually, he had been a ballroom pianist (in the time of the tsar and Sivachev's waltzes), and then he'd become an accompanist. In '17, every kind of dance music had come to a halt for the time being in Old Russia; they played something more martial, and Ivan Ivanovich did a little accompanying here and there. Now Ivan Ivanovich worked in the bookkeeping department of a furniture business.

Kondurin himself and his wife were not quite your run-of-the-mill people; Billancourt doesn't often see people like them. In their past life, both had had lofty experiences, of the most ideal order, so to speak: Ivan Ivanovich had taken one class at the conservatory and not once, not twice, not just three times, had accompanied singers on stage to a packed hall. Alexandra Pavlovna had nearly excelled in a different area: once she got the idea of writing a modest story on an engaging topic drawn from the moods of a woman's soul. Where did she get the nerve? She sent it to the editorial office of a newspaper in the capital and—she called the story "Mitka"!—that was the last she ever saw of it. The editors had the cheek not to publish the story, and they neither returned her manuscript nor entered into any correspondence with her on the subject. But this unfortunate incident had had absolutely no effect on Alexandra Pavlovna's personality.

Ivan Ivanovich looked at his hands. He was a musician. He knew when to add a trill, how to cross his right hand over his left, how to make a fist and run his thumbnail across the keys, like a rag, to the very top notes—all this in the time of the tsar and Sivachev's waltzes. Later, Ivan Ivanovich nearly perished, and later still he was evacuated with a small amount of baggage and in Paris took this job in the furniture business. That had been a little over two years ago.

"It really is a tragedy, Shurochka," he used to say sometimes on Sundays, "a tragedy, darling, that I work in a furniture business instead of doing my own work. I have a God-given talent, I've been a part of the arts all my life, but now history has flung me into economic servitude, and I've had to take a job in the bookkeeping department."

"A tragedy, no doubt about it," Alexandra Pavlovna usually replied from the kitchen. "Fate is playing games with you, a refugee."

Then they would move on to more practical topics of conversation.

One Sunday, though, after he had made quite a few personal acquaintances in Billancourt, Ivan Ivanovich turned the conversation with his wife in a more general political direction:

"Look," he said, "I see now I'm not the only one this tragedy is happening to. This, that, and the other Billancourt resident has wound up where he shouldn't and is burying his talent. It turns out we share a common tragedy. Fate has played the exact same game with Peter Ivanovich, Gerasim Gavrilovich, and Grigory Andreevich."

You couldn't say this thought made Ivan Ivanovich feel any better about his job in the furniture business, though. Not a bit. Quite the opposite, even. He was starting to lose patience, in a certain sense, on Sundays.

And so it happened that Ivan Ivanovich and his boss went to a big furniture auction. They left right after breakfast, one rather unremarkable, rainy day.

At the auction, the babel of all the different junk dealers was inordinate. They were carrying stacks of porcelain toilet fixtures from one hall, shaking rugs out in another, they were bidding in the third for a flue and a bronze dog into the bargain. Ivan Ivanovich fell behind his boss and started roaming the rooms. He had to squeeze by the secretaries, the upholstered furniture begging for new stuffing, a bed that had been standing there for ages, as if rooted to the spot, the balusters for its satin drapes eaten by worms.

In the corner, Ivan Ivanovich saw a piano which, after the death of Viscount A., was going under the hammer with all the rest of his goods and chattel. Anyone who felt like it could try a key: a young lady walked up, bent her knees a little, and there were a couple of notes from some prelude by Rachmaninoff; or a gentleman—a vulgar man, of course—played a fox trot as fast as you've ever heard one; or some cretin would casually drum out a French ditty.

Ivan Ivanovich was amazed at how nonchalant the public was and quietly walked out. He saw another piano, in a second room, and no one around. "You know," he thought, "I'll just try a Sivachev waltz." He walked up, lifted the cover, and . . .

Only the keyboard of this damned piano turned out to be locked; this instrument's inspection wasn't starting until the next day.

Just then, Ivan Ivanovich's boss called to him, took him upstairs, and instructed him in what to do, how they could work together to knock the price down little by little. Once they'd agreed on everything, both entered the auction. Before three hours had passed they had two armchairs, a small elegant marquetried table, an Henri II bookcase, and a cupboard with a secret hiding place.

That evening, Ivan Ivanovich went home, thought it over, and started stroking his hands. "Can't these hands overcome my tragedy?" he thought. "Isn't there some way for me to do what I'm supposed to?"

The smallest silence of any kind upset Alexandra Pavlovna terribly.

"What are you doing in there? What are you thinking about?"

Ivan Ivanovich had no secrets from his wife.

"I saw a piano at the auction today," he said. "It would be

good to get back to my real work, Shurochka. It would be good to find a job somewhere in music, darling."

She sat down opposite him, and they ladled a little soup into their plates.

"As long as I've known you," she said, "you've been struggling against the current, going against the grain. You should get back to your real work, no matter what the cost."

"But what if it was over a long time ago, darling? What if it's all used up, and now—please, step right up!—I should be summoning all my strength for a new life."

These were all disturbing questions, and Ivan Ivanovich was prepared to repeat them to himself endlessly in every key. He thought the general change in Billancourt ought to start with him: he would give up the furniture business, find a job in music, and this incident would put an end to the general unsettledness, everyone would find his own real life for himself. He felt as if he'd been marked out for this from above.

That night, as he lay in bed, the victory he was imagining got him thoroughly worked up. He arose quietly, wearing only his nightshirt, and walked over to the window—it might have been twenty years since he'd walked over to the window at night. He looked: the moon was racing in the sky, the clouds were passing over Paris like white smoke, there was the familiar black smokestack rising between the stars. He felt like taking a big swallow of air—my God, what air this was of theirs at night. It had been years since he'd tasted it! He opened the window and felt a fresh breeze around his legs. He looked out. A pedestrian was passing, weaving, singing a Russian song, "In the Meadows." You could hear him for a long time. The breeze was blowing softly—well, just like in April!

"What are you doing standing there all quiet?" asked Alexandra Pavlovna, who had woken up.

"I don't know. I felt like it. I'll be lying down now," he answered.

And he did.

He dreamed an ideal version of his past, and he arose in the morning gloomy from his dreams.

The evening his fate finally turned around, he was sitting by the window and avidly taking in everything going on before him. Something of the utmost gravity and consequence seemed to be happening to all the people on the street: a little girl was running—to the pharmacy perhaps? Someone was probably dying. . . . No point in the girl wearing out her little feet, the pharmacies are closed today. . . . Two men were saying goodbye on the corner—wasn't that one over there, the tall one, going to prison? They were taking too long to shake hands. It was true, the time had come for him to serve his sentence. . . . And two women, two clever women, were gossiping by the gate just for show: one was about to splash sulfuric acid in the other's face. We know those conversations!

Lowering his eyes, Ivan Ivanovich saw on his knees the morning paper, and in it too were intimations of disaster and opportunity in the world: one scoundrel was searching for another through a classified advertisement with the secret intention of breaking into a bank; in Antwerp they'd invented a new cannon, a kind that shoots by itself; from South Pole to North they were telegraphing about a lost dog. And so forth, so much that everything began to get blurry. And here someone was ringing the doorbell. Was it a fire? . . .

No, it was our famous businessman Semyon Nikolaevich

Kozlobabin, Ivan Ivanovich's old acquaintance, come for a visit.

Semyon Nikolaevich Kozlobabin, to Alexandra Pavlovna's satisfaction, got right down to business. He had decided to open a small but cozy cabaret with twelve tables, to summon up memories of their beautiful past. A place where, apart from everything else, you could have a drink and real Russian porter without any gimmicks, and tea from Russian glasses (there's a place you can get those kinds of glasses), and a shot of our favorite fortified wine. And both to please his weak-chested brother recently arrived from the homeland, and for his own benefit, Kozlobabin had decided to pep up the cabaret with music: to everyone's amazement, his brother had turned out to be a violinist.

Semyon Nikolaevich took a look at Ivan Ivanovich, spun his wedding ring on the table like a top, and said, "What do you think, dear friend, do you still have the divine spark in you? Won't you play the part of pianist in my enterprise?"

This was the direct route to victory over Kondurin's many years of tragedy.

And from that day on, the furniture business continued to flourish, but without him.

The cabaret of our well-known businessman smelled strongly of oil paint at first. The walls were painted gray, tables were installed and a zinc-coated bar. They sat Madame Kozlobabina behind the bar, and they hired someone to wait on tables and another to wash dishes. They leased an upright piano and announced in the newspapers that on Saturdays and Sundays there would be a few gypsy pieces played at this spot on the globe, and on the other nights, free music (violin and piano), and possibly choral performances by the public itself.

The people began to throng in, coming thick and fast to hear the violin, piano, and gypsy singing. For the beginning of the program, the weak-chested brother of our famous business-man performed something separate, from his own repertoire, more or less serious. Then Ivan Ivanovich played a waltz, actu-ally the waltz gushed out from under his fingers. When the waltz was over, they played all kinds of things together, not uncoupling anymore, to the audience's general satisfaction. And then Dunia came up to the piano (I'm not going to tell you any details about this Dunia, even if I have to bite off my tongue!), and this Dunia touched each and every person from the very first couplet, so much did it affect everyone there:

> *A beautiful small corner*
> *We have in Billancourt,*
> *Our fatherland we mourn there,*
> *Each day and every hour!!!*

By this time the weak-chested brother would be trying to get a bite to eat, and Alexandra Pavlovna Kondurina, unable to stand her domestic quiet and solitude, would show up to hear her hus-band.

Of course, Ivan Ivanovich's pay dropped during this time, but then only a memory remained of his tragedy. He didn't get up in the morning at all but rather in the afternoon and imme-diately went to the cabaret to practice all kinds of popular tunes. He was drawn irresistibly to keeping in step with his era. His dinner was whatever God sent, usually soup. And here, of course, Alexandra Pavlovna's ideal past had an effect as well, for she was perfectly content with this turn for the better in her womanly fate.

Ivan Ivanovich was to climb much higher on the ladder of

the arts, however. Among the cabaret's visitors there was an individual possessed of considerable power and, on top of that, of French descent.

This individual (of the male sex, by the way), carried away by the playing on the instruments and Dunia's singing, as well as having drunk a glass or two of we won't say exactly what kind of strong wine, out of the blue struck up a conversation with Ivan Ivanovich and confessed some very interesting things.

First of all, it turned out there was absolutely no reason to be shy with Monsieur Denis, that is, there was nothing at all to be embarrassed about: his ancestor may have sung ballads in Russia in 1789 for all he knew. What he did know was that after the revolution here (there was one) he had gone to Petersburg, where he had worked hard not to fail. What his sons and grandsons did was never mentioned. Maybe they worked in an auto plant, too, or as drivers, in fact they probably did. But his great-grandsons returned to France, and Monsieur Denis was descended from them. Thus, Monsieur Denis's ancestor turned out to be one of us.

In the second place, this same Monsieur Denis, the dear man, the great-great-grandson of someone who sang French gypsy ballads in Old Russia, had a cinema in Billancourt and was offering Kondurin a job in that cinema playing the piano. I have a real artist there plucking away at the cello, he said. He's been doing it for forty years. And your material well-being, he said, would be relatively secure.

Ivan Ivanovich had no secrets from his wife.

"What do you think, darling," he said. "Don't you think our old friend's cabaret might just be a bivouac on life's path? And if you're aiming higher, you have to grab the bull by the horns."

"You know," she replied, "since we've decided to start, we should dig deeper. When it comes to pure art, I think there's more of it in the cinema than a tavern."

So Ivan Ivanovich extricated himself from his position, said his goodbyes to the Kozlobabin brothers and the Kozlobabin wife, found his place in the cinema owner's orchestra, and started playing what he was supposed to.

This was a very special time, and anyone who has never experienced it cannot judge. Ivan Ivanovich even let his hair grow out a little at the neck and bought a turn-down collar for Fridays, Saturdays, and Sundays. On Monday he dressed simply, in what he used to wear to the furniture business. On Monday the turn-down collar was laundered, on Tuesday ironed, and on Wednesday and Thursday it lay in his bureau, wrapped in a clean handkerchief.

On the days of the first performances, after lunch, there was rehearsal. First they ran through the film and chose motifs for it, simple motifs that hit the drama's nail on the head. Then they started playing with the next performers who entertained the audience during the entr'acte.

There were Japanese jugglers, and there were singers of satirical songs, mediocre young men who looked like spongers. There were dancing girls whose toes pointed either at Ivan Ivanovich's ear or his tooth—truth be told, there were all kinds of things here.

Before a week had passed Ivan Ivanovich had acquired new friends, divinely sweet-faced artists who had not buried but had plied their talent for all it was worth. A bespectacled young lady played the violin; her future was secure because of that fiddle. On the cello was the same artist I've already told you about, and on the viola a mild little man who, in spite of his appearance, had easily put six children on their feet and started them off in the same direction. This orchestra also had assistance (on Fridays, Saturdays, and Sundays) from a solid man who took charge of the doublebass, kettledrum, and snare all at the same time. He was a positive specialist, the likes of whom you might not find more than five of in the whole world.

Alexandra Pavlovna was given a free ticket in the first row. Ivan Ivanovich showed up before everyone else, ten minutes before the performance started, checked the lighting, and gave the tobacco on the keyboard a swipe with a rag—tobacco had been dropped on the piano by the last pianist and now was gradually coming out of every crack, like some kind of nasty trick. People started filling the hall, taking their seats, coughing, rustling newspapers, cracking nuts. The young lady and the viola arrived; there might even have been something going on between them, he didn't know. Gramps arrived with his cello and blew his nose with a honking sound. A shudder ran through Ivan Ivanovich, a sacred quiver. Would he give the A to the right or the left? The audience began to stir. One last draft ran through Kondurin's long hair. And when the orchestra played the march-overture, it played as one man.

Outside a light rain was falling and maybe some down-and-outer was getting wet, maybe someone's fondest dreams were not coming true, maybe someone felt like borrowing a little money, or simply taking it without giving it back. Or maybe questions were starting to occur to someone: it would be good just to be doing what you were supposed to do, it would be good if, for example, there was an end to all the tragedy in Billancourt. It would be good if it suddenly turned out that there had been no Perekop, no evacuation, that they hadn't retreated through the swamps or contracted typhus in Rostov.

The march-overture roared, and Alexandra Pavlovna in the first row got ready to watch the dramatic film. The wages, of course, were less, the furniture business paid more, but this lady had not experienced suffering of an elevated nature in the past for nothing. Outside, I'm telling you, there could have been fog at this time of year, or a wind, someone could have been terribly jealous of Ivan Ivanovich and wanted to outdo him in well-being. No matter what, he would do his utmost. Maybe outside there was tuberculosis or despair, maybe something far worse. Maybe—forgive me for saying so, readers and customers—someone was planning to steal something. Billancourt was not exactly your dacha community; all sorts of things happened here.

A month passed, then two. Winter announced itself. Christmas was drawing near, anyone could see that. As Christmas approached, the cinematographic institution could have stood a little white paint, a harp drawn on the ceiling or a border down the wall, so that everything would be ready in advance for the new year of 1930, so that this 1930 could be lived honorably. Already a lot of people were starting to give this careful thought.

Only don't believe in renovations, my dears. The way we do it, repairs always conceal some trick. Don't believe newly hung wallpaper and repainted walls, don't trust the whitewashing of ceilings or new parquet floors. If today they're sweeping out your trash, tomorrow they could be sweeping you out, too.

The first painters arrived on Monday morning and started with the offices in the back. These were quiet men, polite and neat. The boss, the descendant of those Frenchmen who once in Petersburg, like us sinners, had sung French gypsy ballads, did not let them out of his sight and ran around them with empty hands. But the painters worked slowly (albeit steadily). On Saturday they had still not started on the main hall. That was when it was decided to shut the enterprise down for two weeks, so that there would be no interference from the public whatsoever in internal matters.

The beauty was going to be brought out in full: the chairs cleaned and renumbered, a new curtain cut and a new uniform designed for the employees. All kinds of insane plans roamed around in the owner's mind. And on Saturday he decided to share them with his orchestra.

He addressed them in French. "I am not some kind of ostrich, hiding my head from you under my wing," he said. "I am giving you money in advance, as much as the law requires. I'm installing mechanical music. First, it's an economy, second, the parterre will increase by three rows, and three, it's the modern way. I'm very happy to have known you all."

He said this before the performance. Right before. That day the specialist was there, too, the kind of man you could hardly find ten of anywhere on the planet.

"But where are we to go?" the specialist said softly.

"Ah," he said, "the same place where the singers of satirical songs and the jugglers are going. I'm handing them their hats, too, because now they too are seriously not modern."

Then the artist who had been sawing away on the cello for forty years spoke up.

"Is that really the same thing—our music and a mechanical gramophone? It's the same as if"—here he took a deep breath,

he was so upset—"instead of the wife you'd lived with for forty
years you suddenly took up with some flibbertigibbet you'd
picked up for two rubles fifty!"

Ivan Ivanovich silently ran his hand through his hair, which
had already started curling up a little. Then he walked over to
his piano, and together they played their swan song—the
march-overture.

"Shurochka," he said when he was home and slowly
undressing in the middle of the room, "we've been caught by
history once again. And this time we're not alone either, I'm
telling you, darling. You realize, this is a complication. We
need to think it through, it's hard to know what to say. Besides
you and me, and our dear friends, other new people have land-
ed here—one respected gentleman, and another very decent
man, and a young lady. Our tragedy affects other people, too, it
turns out. We and our dear friends apparently are not alone,
we're part of something bigger."

"If that's the case," said Alexandra Pavlovna, "then the
thought is some consolation. It makes it easier if you're not
alone. You've swum against the current enough in your life."

"That's something we need to think about, too. It may be
easier, but it may not. It means there's nowhere for a man to go
if even the gentleman and the young lady . . . It looks like it's
going to be harder after all, darling."

At this point it was time to turn off the light.

Perhaps someone will take an interest in the subsequent
fate of Ivan Ivanovich, perhaps someone for one brief moment
will worry that he might have perished. No. Not at all. Many
of those who dream of Monsieur Renault on a rainy day on the
Place Nationale might even envy him. He went back to the fur-

niture business, to his old position (by that time Kozlobabin's cabaret had closed down, as had many of those cabarets of late). That is, the very same position he had held for more than two years.

And it can be said with confidence that unless something utterly impossible happens in our world, something utterly incredible, unless it gets like it was in the old days or even worse, Ivan Ivanovich will never quit this job again. He will lose his patience once or twice during his idle hours but will take no action whatsoever. Because the tragedy, it turned out, was not just his, mine, and yours, but a common tragedy, universal even.

That's it exactly—universal. Forgive me the discouraging word.

1929

A Gypsy Romance

"Grisha, let's drink to that charming Parisian Irochka!"

"Petya, let's drink to that charming Parisian Olga Fyodorovna!"

In the street that crosses ours, very close to the black river, night begins at nine o'clock and lasts until four. Such are our customs and ways. At nine o'clock the moon comes out from behind the apartment buildings—not every day, no one would believe that—but when it does, it comes out gray, plump, and flabby and shines on the cross street, shines on the crimson and ginger street lamps. What a scene! What beauty!

The Hungarian kept the curtains drawn in his establishment. A duo played the mandolin and guitar, and anyone who wanted to listen had to pay. The duo played to the glory of the owner, the owner who had two wives in South America working for him. He was fat and he was rich.

Two wives, and a third whom he had brought only as far as Paris. Here she had taken a walk through the streets one day, never to be seen again. She had had red hair that hung halfway down her back, breasts no dress could conceal, and a low, plaintive voice. She had stepped out to take a breath of Parisian air and had never returned to the establishment. People said the insurance company had given the Hungarian money for his wife.

He was fat, he was rich, and his tables were wooden and stained with wine. The mandolin and the guitar sat in the corner near the counter. They were dirty and hairy and had big noses and bass voices. Smoke hung in the air, and a solitary young woman sat in the smoke, silent, waiting for customers.

"Grisha, let's drink to the charming Parisian Lyalechka!"

"Petya, let's drink to the charming Parisian Vera Dmitrievna!"

The windows were sweating from all the heavy drinking; the walls and doors were sticky. The voices were getting noisier and noisier, people were moving closer together, damp hair was falling into eyes, hands were grabbing mugs, chairs, knives. Two men lunged at one another. When the killing started, the lights went off and the clients and musicians were driven out. The dead man was carried out onto the pavement, set down in the gutter, and the doors were locked. Enough for one day!

The dead man lay doubled over, hatless, but wearing his coat. People—maybe even you and I—walked past and said: "Got himself drunk, the shameless devil, lying in the gutter like some genius." It was growing light. The moment something flashed in the sky—you couldn't tell from which direction—a passerby, if he wasn't too lost in thought, would see the thick gloom in the face of the lying man, and mindful of his duties as a citizen and resident would go to the nearest café and make an anonymous telephone call to the police station.

Its sirens screeching for two blocks, and barely making the turn into the cross street, a tall panel truck pulled up next to the corpse. There was no one and nothing around. The music had stopped a long time ago, and eight men, cheerful, well-fed, and well-groomed, family men wearing blue uniforms, jumped down to the pavement. Fewer than that never came to this street. It just wasn't done.

Above, from the upper floors, several captivating little heads poked out, their nightshirts slipping off their shoulders, and from inside their smelly rooms, irritated bass voices barked peremptorily.

They took the man away and never printed anything about him in the newspapers. People in the neighborhood might get angry, because then no one would want to rent apartments or open stores there.

But whoever moved there lived there. Breathed the fumes. Someone doing business there would never close up for anything: the light stayed on til midnight, and there were prices on the pies and shirts. What if some Chinaman needed to buy a tie that night, or some young lady got a sudden urge to buy a bandage?

"Grisha, let's drink to the charming Parisian Tanechka!"

"Petya, let's drink to the charming Parisian Maria Petrovna!"

Catercorner from the Hungarian's, slant-eyed, yellow-faced men were shooting craps, and the white faces in their company were having a hard time staying awake. Only three of them held out, three short and not very fancy females, who refused to give up their seats. They'd been sitting along those walls for years. Under favorable circumstances, they might have had children by those Chinamen, and those children might have been school age by now.

Sometimes it happened that a shrill cry would go up from the tables, and one man would throw himself on another and wrap his five fingers around the other man's throat. But it never stopped at two here. A third would step in, and after the third, a fourth. Their shouts were short, jerky, and nasal, the doors and windows were wide open and there weren't any curtains. And then people walking down the street would dash in where it was a little brighter, where lamps gleamed with tidiness, where . . . well, in short, people were looking for something a little better than that crossstreet.

Not far away, on the third floor, lived a young man who had already coughed out one lung—an insignificant part of himself—without anyone ever noticing. He had given himself bedsores lying there, and his thigh had opened and was oozing, but his mama was gone and he was all alone. His window was open because the doctor had ordered him to breathe what he could, and from his bed he looked out the window—at the bar. There wasn't a mandolin or guitar, or even yellow faces, actually, there were *gray faces* sitting there, and a piano being played. And a woman of indescribable bounty and loveliness sang gypsy songs there on Billancourt holidays. The young man was sweating, trying to hang on to his last lung, and he would stare at the windows of that bar until he felt like crying.

Oh, Dunia, what Black Sea *gymnasium* robbed you of your golden childhood?

He looked down on the two rows of tables covered with patterned white paper, at the red wallpaper, at the counter behind which the tall bearded nobleman busied himself, at the man, whose head he couldn't see, playing the piano. All he could see were hands hammering on the keys, and a portrait of a general, or maybe it was an admiral, nailed to the wall. He looked at the slit in the black dress, the ornate shawl, the large bronze gypsy hands with apricot nails. The dying man's clarity of vision amazed the doctor who was treating him for bedsores, hysteria, and sweating; the doctor, was not even attempting to treat his tuberculosis.

Oh, Dunia, why don't you ever look up, into the gloom, at the window, into these two eyes twitching from lack of sleep?

She tapped out the rhythm with her heel and shimmied her soft shoulders occasionally. The pianist played the waltzes to which our fathers surrendered Port Arthur. She took a faded rose from the glass on the table and scratched the end of her nose with it, humming *trum-trum-trum* so that her soul exuded sorrow and self-pity. This rose was the business's rose, their rose, so she couldn't pin it to her breast or stick it behind her ear.

When a client came in, alone usually, rarely with a lady, she would give him the once-over and then pass her eyes over his face a couple of times, as if in hopes of encountering some kind of miracle in that unworthy visage. And each time she took the not very fresh rose away from her face, so that she would appear in all her splendor. And each time she tossed her hair back with infuriating nonchalance and hummed *trum-trum-trum*.

Then the dignified nobleman would start running quickly back and forth behind the counter, wiping up something that left a stain on his rag. The nobleman's eyes bored into the arrivals, and his beard, the legacy of better, albeit troubled times, seemed to make the lower half of his skinny face look scruffy.

"What would you like?"

"What do you have?"

"Sardines and onion."

"What about tea?"

"Yes, naturally."

"And vodka?"

"Quite so."

"Ah. . . ."

A minute passed. A rich chord played on the piano, long, but not too loud.

"Do you have blini?"

"Have mercy!"

"What about shish kebab?"

"Hee hee, very sorry."

"Well, then, in that case give me a carafe filled with what it should be, and *madame* would like a cutlet."

The pianist struck the keys as if he wanted to smash the instrument to pieces.

"In the Hills of Manchuria," "Alyosha!" "Two Guitars," "Ramona," "Little Bubliks," "Alyosha!" "Why Did I Have to Fall in Love," "Dark Eyes," "Toy Blocks," "Ramona," "Alyosha!"

The pedal droned when it was pressed, forming a bridge from the last notes of the two guitars to the little *bubliks*, vague phrases without end or beginning, in couplets of a temperament distinctly not local. In those few seconds when the pianist threw back his head, as if overcome by the piercing notes, you might hear this:

"There is a country where elephants make way for flies, but for now, if you've got a wallet, hold on tight."

"What makes you think I have so much money today, lads?"

"But I lent you two and a half, Ignaty Savelievich Bodrov."

The door opened yet again, and in the stream of clean night

air walked a tall, clean-shaven man wearing pince-nez. He had on a coat, the kind we used to call a covert coat in Russia, and a hat in the very latest style, made of some kind of fuzzy material. He walked in confidently, chose a seat next to the mirror, and sat down. He took a cheap cigarette out of his wooden cigarette case, tapped it, and lit up. Scratched on the wooden cigarette case in gold letters was this: "Marriage is the heart's prison." Out of habit the man read either the last word or the first. And eloquently contemplated that word.

Dunia noticed the newcomer and suddenly her eyes looked different, a little drunk, and her lips parted slightly. She threw down the rose and walked over. She blocked out the rest of the room with her body, leaned her breasts toward the guest, and asked, "White? Red? What's kept you away so long?"

"White."

"You haven't been here for a whole month. What should they play for you?"

"Whatever they like."

"Shall I sing for you? I thought you were never coming back."

She lingered near him until her face was burning. The nobleman hurriedly readied a carafe of white wine. The floor shifted under Dunia, and the governor on the wall seemed to sway.

She sang what you would expect, then served people their wine, and then she and the nobleman counted up the Cossack cutlets, Hamburg and country steaks, the hussar liver sauté—everything that had been eaten at dinner. (Even Lent didn't air out the smell of those cutlets and that hussar liver.) Then, distracted, she sat down at the table where people she had known for a long time were sitting, people who were practically fami-

ly, and she danced a foxtrot with one of these near-relations to
"Little Bubliks," displaying her buxom figure to all around
until everyone started feeling light-headed. But she did not take
her eyes off the visitor in the hat.

He was smoking, sitting perfectly still. He looked out of
place—too intellectual and calm. He liked the commotion and
the red wallpaper, and every once in a while (Leave me alone!)
he must have picked up that thick glass (I'm sick of it all!).

"Aren't you going to say something to me?"

"What should I say?"

She sat down next to him, suddenly forgetting everything
else.

"Did you go away?"

"No."

"Why didn't you keep your promise?"

"That's why promises are made, to be broken."

He thought for a moment and chuckled.

"What are those earrings you're wearing? You didn't have
those before, did you?"

She leaned toward him, holding her breath. A green glass
drop mounted in gold fell on her cheek. She placed her large,
swarthy hand on the table to see whether the vein in her wrist
was throbbing. But her hand was perfectly calm.

"What was that you said? Promises. . . .?"

He smiled but didn't answer.

"Do you have someone now?"

"When I have money, God always sends someone."

"Why did you come today?"

He looked around, pleased.

"I like to observe, I always have. Billancourt isn't Paris,

Billancourt is unlike anywhere else in the whole world. It's a fascinating study. Take you, for instance. Why not learn a thing or two?"

She frowned at him. There was a nasty expression on her face.

"How much do I owe?" he asked.

She pushed back her chair and wrote his check with a pencil stub on the paper tablecloth. He paid, stood up, and left.

She took the money to the nobleman, walking to the beat of the music, then wrapped her shawl around her chest and went out as well.

The guest was walking away, striding straight down the street. He was walking fast, waving his cane. He was going in the direction of the city, although all directions here are good.

Very far away, behind the closed shutters of a corner building, Polish workmen were singing their national anthem in a tuneful chorus. Stars were hanging in the sky, and the moon was crossing overhead, the useless tin moon. Amid the bricks of an unfinished building a man and a woman were arguing. The sidewalks were deserted. Dunia very quietly watched the man turn the corner. Across the way an irrelevant clanging trolley passed by.

From his third-floor window, the dying dreamer watched her. If he stretched, he could see that very length of sidewalk where Dunia had stopped in a strip of light. On the street she always seemed shorter to him than when she was inside among the tables. There she seemed so robust, the floor should have quaked under her feet. Here, all wrapped up, watching someone walk away, she was young, light-footed, and defenseless.

He knew exactly what he could see in the frame of his open window, from the low-slung star that certainly must have had a name and the smokestacks under it that belched smoke until the dinner hour, to the opposite sidewalk, stained with spit and worse, of this dark cross street, where the only time you could sleep was during the day. Only he couldn't sleep anymore without raving, and when he raved, he woke the landlady, who sat downstairs in constant twilight, upset by his cries.

Dunia walked straight down the street. The evening was warm, a spring evening. Very close by, perhaps in the garden of the community school, flowers were in bloom. You could see the trees through the fence; the street there was paved with cobblestones and reminded our brother of something. That can happen when it smells of a slow spring and the acacias' white flowers are blooming. And if it's quiet and sad, and there's no one around, then it brings back powerful memories. Of a district town. To each his own.

Dunia almost started running. The Hungarian's third wife probably ran through these parts the same way—she just wanted to take a walk and get a little air, see where the river was and the cinema and where they sold buttons. She walked out proudly and then she too nearly started running, she turned the corner—and it was all over. People said that they fished a ginger-haired woman out of the river, but that wasn't in Billancourt. Later people said they'd seen someone who looked like her in a fancy building—we all know which one—but she swore she didn't understand Hungarian.

Turning the corner, Dunia didn't stop. On the contrary, she sped up as much as she could and headed down toward the embankment.

"Listen," she shouted. "There's something I have to tell you."

The man with the cane halted. He touched his fuzzy hat with two fingers. He was a polite man, obviously quite cultured.

Dunia ran across the street and stopped in front of him. There was a path under the trees here, right at the water's edge. The water rustled, glittered. It was easy to tell that Dunia had not thought anything through properly. She saw the man in front of her and trembled all over—nothing more.

He was getting ready to ask her about something, or maybe just looked like he was. She made a sudden movement, and he guessed she was going to spit in his face. He grabbed her by the arms to make sure she wasn't carrying a weapon. She wasn't. "Oh you . . ." he said nastily and slapped her across the face. She bumped the hat from his head, knocked off his pince-nez, and clutched at his hair, which was rather thick and pleasant to the touch.

"You can go to hell!" he exclaimed softly and flung her aside. She didn't fall when she ran into the tree.

He took a step toward her, crushing his pince-nez on the path, and dragged her toward the water's edge. He should have left. She pushed him, but he stopped her. She shoved him in the chest again. He let her go with a curse that was actually shocking: that such a fine man should have picked up something like that.

The young man on the third floor stretched toward the window so hard his joints cracked.

He was used to the limits of his observations, he could grumble at the gods as much as he liked but it would make no difference. The sound of voices, dishes, and music reached him from downstairs. A door slammed, songs were sung, people danced and banged on the piano keys. Windows were rattling, dogs waking up in courtyards, cats yowling on roofs.

It hurt him to touch his own body, he kept his arms spread wide and sweated. Sometimes he summoned all his strength and took the towel from his headboard to wipe his brow, the back of his neck, his chest, his wet palms. After this he would take a few minutes to rest with his eyes closed. Then he would gaze down again at the headless revelry, at the two rows of tables in disarray, and at the portrait (God save the tsar!) of the governor-general.

Suddenly a shot rang out somewhere. Shooting on the eve of a holiday is nothing special. None of us gets excited about shooting. It wasn't a loud shot. It came from the direction of the bridge, some drunk had probably taken a pot shot at a streetlamp—they liked doing that.

Dunia was walking down the cross street, this time on the sidewalk. She's a vigorous one, our Dunia, and when she walks you can hear her. She was carrying her ornate shawl, which was torn to shreds. But Dunia looked perfectly decent—I mean, not decent but ordinary. She had taken the time to fix herself up.

She stopped for a moment before she reached the doors to make sure she was herself again. She was being watched from the hotel across the way, but she didn't see that. The hotel was like our Caprice, I think it was called the Surprise. It was just another building, an ordinary one people slept in.

Arm in arm, as if preparing to attack, some Italians were walking down the street making a cheerful racket. Trying to sing three-part harmony, they emphasized the words of passion: there were *sole* and *mare* and *amore*. Actually, what wasn't there? Some were imitating different instruments with their mouths, they were playing in an orchestra, and they didn't care about anyone or anything. Dunia waited for them to pass.

And the young man on the third floor waited too, and then he said:

> *For flashing eyes' enchanting gaze*
> *I fear not torture, or heavy chains.*

She shuddered and raised her head—and thought she would burst into tears.

"Senichka, is that you? What are you scaring me for? I can't see anyone."

"No, it's not Senichka," said a quiet voice at the window with melancholy alarm. "What Senichka is that? Were you expecting Senichka? No, I'm not Senichka. Did you want Senichka?"

It was quiet on the street now. The man and woman had finished fighting by the walls of the unfinished building and now slept on the ground in each other's embrace, on boards that had been piled there the night before and so were dry. The wind rose from across the river, carrying with it the smells of the happy nighttime city. If it weren't for the Paris wind we'd have nothing to breathe in Billancourt. It blows cunningly, it blows subtly, sometimes suffocating you, sometimes with an intriguing but unwholesome freshness that relaxes you, that chases away all sleep, dreams, and intoxication. They should ban it from blowing on us. But how would we ever get along without Paris? It's inconceivable. Your soul aches to meet that wind head on.

"Grisha, let's drink to the charming Parisian Zhenechka!"

"Petya, let's drink to the charming Parisian Klavdia Sergeevna!"

A third carafe was brought for someone. Dunia went back
to the tables, the nobleman, and the rose. They were waiting for
her. In the time she'd been running through the streets a chorus had gathered in the corner, a chorus that was practically
family. Only she was missing.

"Grisha, let's drink to the charming . . ."

" . . . the charming Parisian. . ."

1930

The Little Stranger

Anastasia Georgievna Seyantseva had lived in Billancourt
from time immemorial—nine years at the very least. She
had arrived when construction was being completed on the
Hotel Caprice and was the first to move in, for which the
Caprice's owner gave her a prize: a flowerpot of unbreakable
marble, which she picked up by one handle and placed on her
mantel. She remembered when the first foreign guests showed
up on the Place Nationale. They huddled in clusters on the
ground: the crying children were half-naked; the women were
unwashed, ragged, bareheaded, bear-legged, with frightened,
glistening eyes; and the gloomy men, unshaven and wearing
English-style overcoats, sat nearby, never taking their eyes off
the pathetic parcels they had dragged all across Europe, bulging
with kettles, icons, and boots.

At first the local population called the newcomers gypsies,
and later, after long arguments over the peoples of the East,
Poles, but then it came out that these starving refugees were not
of the French faith. Then people seized on the notion that they
were Serbs: Serbs were preordained to drain the bitterest dregs.

People had been insulting Serbs for as long as anyone could remember.

But the Parisian reporters came with their notebooks, pencils, and cameras and declared (they knew it!) that these people were Armenians who had fled from outside Trebizond across Mesopotamia and who had been brought here to Billancourt to lend Monsieur Renault a hand.

The neighborhood bistro owners started bringing out big cups of bouillon made from cubes for the foreigners, as well as hunks of bread. The children clung to their mothers with both hands, and the mothers with both hands clung to the cups.

"Are you Armenian?" they were asked. But they just shook their heads and said thank you.

One day, Anastasia Georgievna Seyantseva, who had scarcely left the Caprice since arriving the month before, was walking by. She asked why these unsanitary people were sitting on the ground when there were benches? And she was told they were ashamed.

She walked up to one of the women who was rocking an infant, shifting him from arm to arm. She had just nursed him, and her breast was bared. The infant had been born about a week before and had probably still not been registered at the Billancourt City Hall. Anastasia heard the woman croon:

Tri-ta-tashki tri-ta-tish,
First on that one, then on this.

Anastasia Georgievna looked at the breast that had been dragged all across Europe and felt something warm fill her eyes and even spill over her eyelids and run down her cheek, something people might notice. She went to the bistro owners, took out a little of the money she kept in her traveling bag, and asked them to put a piece of meat in each cup of bouillon.

Everyone was amazed. Is this really the Russians? The very same? Who would have expected it!

Under the tsar's regime, Anastasia Georgievna had been a cheerful, flirtatious *young thing*. She had been married but had treated her husband badly and preferred traveling abroad, with a lady friend or alone. She liked making friends on trains and at resorts. She liked to dress up, flirt and twirl. She preferred flowers to berries, but she was happy with berries, too. In Petersburg, where she spent her winters, she studied singing, played the piano, and the two years before the war, ignoring her inconspicuous husband, chased—with ambushes, threatening letters, and nighttime expectations—the writer Andreev, so that he nearly fell into her hands, but God rescued him.

She dressed with no regard for fashion, wore a curl between her eyebrows and was always opening and closing her coat, bundling up and then letting it fall off her shoulder. . . . In short, she behaved like a captivating enigma. Well, so what, if she had the money!

Due to her height and unusual thinness, as well as her love for all manner of rare poses, she was sometimes taken in public and society (for instance, when she happened to be sitting in an armchair by a window or door) for drapery that had fallen off its hook: very long and covered in material. And all of a sudden the drapery would burst into laughter, or give a quick shake, or stand up and go play some chords. And then everyone would see her pink temples and the curl between her eyebrows. Which many people liked, of course.

No one knows what happened to her during the three years between when the revolution befell us and when she showed up in Billancourt. People said—and just what won't people say?—that her husband had been shot, her money, home, musical instruments, and frippery confiscated, and she had been driven entirely on her own, like an oak leaf, all across Russia, all the way to the Black Sea, where she was hungry and cold and mangy and even lousy. Once she had crossed the Black Sea, she disembarked in the Balkans a completely changed person.

At the time, in '20 or so, she was about forty, but to look at her you'd think she was more. She didn't stay long in the Balkans, but came to Paris. Everything in Paris seemed very expensive to her, so she decided to settle outside the city. People said she still had some money left, but just what won't people say?

It wasn't that her feminine intuition had foretold Billancourt's glorious future. She wound up here by accident: she saw the hotel, took a room, was given the flowerpot, and began living quietly.

When she came out onto the Place Nationale she was a thin woman, still tall, wearing a long, black, mannish coat and a cloth hat of indeterminate style, and at the sides and back you could see her half-light brown, half-gray hair. She held her hands in their crocheted gloves up to her chest, wrists down, and under her arm she had slipped her once quite suitable, now discolored traveling bag. Her feet were rather large and she wore low-heeled patent pumps with a wide flat bow, the kind fops wear with their frock coats and all that other folderol. She held herself erect as she walked. Her face had a grayish-yellow tinge and dry wrinkles; only her temples were still pink; her mouth was always firmly closed, her gaze sharp and piercing.

Her room had an empty feel. There was a mustachioed man wearing a morning coat in a playful frame. On the mantel lay a silver hand mirror, two cans of pomade, a large round box of talcum powder, and an unopened bottle of ink. Often Anastasia Georgievna picked up the mirror and looked into it. The fact that she had lost her looks beyond all measure or that she had aged in the last few years was not what bothered her. What bothered her was the fact that very, very close by, coming nearer and nearer, was her own lonely death. That much she knew.

Back in Bulgaria she had found out she was incurably ill. Nights, her right side ached, and the doctor in Bulgaria had discovered a tumor between her side and the small of her back. She knew there was one operation that might help her, but she did not want to think about it. She realized the day would come when she wouldn't be able to heat water for herself, and the night would come when there would be no one to close her eyes. And then another, now eternal loneliness would come, and there would be no one to weep over the burdock on her grave.

Sitting very quietly in her room, in front of the unexpected flowerpot, she calculated how old her son and daughter might have been if she had not refused to have children during the time of the tsar and her *boudoir.* And how old her parents would be if they were still alive, and her sister. . . . But at this point she broke off her calculations: her sister did exist, she had seen her sister, and they had taken no pleasure in one another.

A month after her arrival in Billancourt, Anastasia Georgievna had found herself employment: she sewed glass eyes on stuffed animals. She also sewed on their whiskers and claws and secured their tails. It was work she did not have to be

ashamed of. Only a not very pleasant smell clung to the room:
a mixture of pomade and plush. In short, the mixture of man
and beast.

The years passed, and those who had been nursed on the
Place Nationale were sent to school; the men had shaved off
their beards and now had something chivalrous about them (on
Sundays!). Billancourt was changing, Billancourt was bending
this way and that, like a blade of grass, in the commercial hands
of Monsieur Renault. The Hotel Caprice filled up, and around
Anastasia Georgievna people started talking, visiting, fussing,
playing balalaikas. Madame Klava started working away on her
sewing machine, and Semyon Nikolaevich Kozlobabin plied his
grocery trade on the corner.

One day, a letter arrived in the evening post for Anastasia
Georgievna from a General Tverdotrubov, whom she had never
heard of before:

Dear Madame!

Allow me to disturb your peace and quiet and tell
you some sad news: your sister, Ekaterina Georgievna
Bryantsovich, passed away a week ago from an ailment
of the heart. Her last will, caught by the keen ear of a
loving heart, was this:

a. To give the property of her apartment to me, as
the person and adviser closest to her.

b. To send her daughter Ekaterina, thirteen years
old, to you, as the closest blood relative.

I hope, my dear, there will be no arguments
between us, since the property has been mine from the
very beginning!!!

"Please be so good as to inform me when you will come for the (departed: crossed out) daughter) so that we can honor the final will of our dear (daughter: crossed out) departed.

> At your service,
> Full General of the Infantry
> Alexei Tverdotrubov.

Anastasia Georgievna turned white, then gray, and barely reached her chair. At first she was pierced by a kind of joy, but then a horrible unease engulfed her: Not for this had she inured herself to her ferocious loneliness all these years, not for this had she reconciled herself to the idea of dying with unclosed eyes, not so that now, suddenly, everything would be violated and her memories of her life as a *young thing* and her habits as a dying woman would go up in smoke. She had not loved her sister, she had only seen her sister abroad one time, and they had taken no pleasure in one another.

All evening she paced like a madwoman, not knowing what to do. She kept seeing before her a stranger, a little girl she'd never met, and a full general, most likely her deceased sister's lover. Judging from the letter, the general could not be a terribly sober man. She did not sleep all night, and in the morning she got up and thought: I can't decide anything, I can't worry about anything, I have to go there and see for myself. She wrote the general that she would come to Paris the next Sunday, at three o'clock. Nothing more.

But something happened on Saturday to upset her plans. At about nine o'clock in the morning, as she was getting ready to go to the workshop to pick up some work, there was a knock at the door. Anastasia Georgievna already had her coat on but had not yet put on her hat. Her hair separated at its part naturally, so that her scalp showed through.

A girl walked in, a tallish, freckled, browless, large-mouthed girl who was a little on the skinny side and almost a redhead. She was carrying a bundle under her arm.

"It's me," she said. "So you wouldn't have to come for me. Hello, aunt."

"Aunt"—that was Anastasia Georgievna. For the first time in her life she was an aunt. Once on the Place Nationale the banana seller had called her auntie: "What're you shovin' for, auntie? See? There's plenty for everyone, with something left over for Monsieur Renault."

"Hello," said Anastasia Georgievna. "Isn't it a little odd you didn't wait for me?"

The girl started mumbling something but then forced herself to answer, and even make eye contact.

"I didn't want you to see how we live."

"How do you live?"

"Not the normal way, people don't live like that. Tverdotrubov's always drunk and bringing in all kinds of people. He tracks in dirt. I spend all day cleaning, but nothing helps."

"A general from the infantry and he's let himself go like that!"

"He's no general. He lost all his money at the races."

The fact that Tverdotrubov turned out not to be a general suddenly clarified Anastasia Georgievna's thoughts.

"Sit down," she said. "Do you think it smells odd in here? I'll open the window. You know, I'm not used to this, I'm kind of an old maid."

"I'm kind of an old maid, too," the girl said, and she sat down.

She was wearing a reddish coat with a black fur collar and a black hat. She crossed her long, in black ribbed stockings, legs under her chair.

She had the look of someone who had made up her mind. Her small dark eyes goggled, she was very pale, and she kept clasping and unclasping her hands, which were red and shiny from laundry and lye. She placed her bundle, which was wrapped in a sheet of newspaper, on the floor beside her.

Anastasia Georgievna was still standing motionless in the middle of the room.

"What about your mama?" she asked indecisively.

"I laid mama out. She died suddenly, no one ever expected it, she washed the floor and died."

"Did she want you to come live with me?"

"No, that was Tverdotrubov's idea. He said it would be better if I didn't stay with him, especially since he had an opportunity to get me off his hands. He's not a mean man, just unusually drunken."

Anastasia Georgievna listened. This was all quite amazing.

"And he's dirty. He comes in and throws everything all around. Especially when he's angry. And he gets angry because he doesn't listen to anyone. Last Sunday I told him only a fool would bet on Tip-Top-Terry. Bet on Anatole France, otherwise you'll be stupidly squandering your last franc. He did what he pleased, though. He bet on Tip-Top-Terry and she came in third, but they were paying seventy-two to five for Anatole France."

Something pricked Anastasia Georgievna's heart.

"Come here and kiss me," and she turned her head to the side.

The girl went up and kissed her, quickly, her lips barely grazing her aunt's cheeks. Anastasia Georgievna held her by the shoulders.

"You're not going to miss your mama, are you?"

"No, I won't."

"What about Tverdotrubov?"

"He's not worth missing."

"You'll get used to living with me, right? It's all a matter of habit."

"Habit, of course."

Anastasia Georgievna leaned toward the girl and felt her breath but did not shudder.

"You're going to work with me and sleep in this room. If you need anything, you'll tell me."

"Thank you very much, I don't need anything, I have everything," and she glanced at the bundle under the chair.

Anastasia Georgievna did not know how to talk to people, and the girl did not tell her any more upsetting stories from her life. She still had the look of someone who has made up her mind to do a lot. Not even at night, in her sleep, did the expression on her little face change. In the mornings she silently straightened the room (she slept on three chairs) and ran out for milk and a roll.

While she was out, Anastasia Georgievna got up. She never arose in front of the girl and in the evening went to bed in total darkness. They sat facing one another and sewed eyes on gorillas and rabbits, and after lunch the same, until evening. Before dinner the girl took the work back (the workshop was not far) and then, while Anastasia Georgievna resewed and recut old skirts, the girl ran through the streets and onto the square, as if she were missing something crucial.

Anastasia Georgievna had plenty to think about in her silence. The girl had long, nimble fingers, she knew how to hold a needle and blow into the eye before threading it. She paced around the room, sometimes coughing softly into her fist. No matter where you looked, there she was, in Anastasia Georgievna's thoughts, too.

Anastasia Georgievna could see that it was getting harder for her to move around every day. Her head would spin, her temperature would go up, and she was always sleepy. The girl's presence gradually altered her thoughts. Her memories of a cheerful loneliness and of her easy life as a *young thing* receded, and her old rash thoughts about burdock drew nigh.

The girl knew how to cook kasha on the primus, how to test a potato with a fork and salt it properly. They bought two cups and saucers. After three years of hunger and mange and a few years of Billancourt, Anastasia Georgievna was indifferent to creature comforts. She had not even come to like them during her long illness, and she did not get attached to things—or people.

All the days were much alike. Today Anastasia Georgievna would gasp in pain as she sat down to work, and tomorrow the girl, as if she had just remembered something, would get lost in thought in the middle of dinner, her spoon still in her hand, or would pause while biting off a thread, sitting by the window and looking at the street, where it was noisy, shabby, and dark. The days passed, the weeks passed, and on Sundays it was the same, only they worked for themselves rather than the workshop: the laundry, a little darning, and then you could hear the water running, the scissors clicking, or the iron hissing.

Anastasia Georgievna did not go out anymore to the square, where the wind blew and the rain fell. She had almost stopped eating. The pains in her side never let up and she had to give up working. Now the girl sat alone at the table, and Anastasia Georgievna lay in bed and silently, always silently, thought.

She thought, actually, about the fact that she was not at all irritable, as the Balkan doctor had warned. Despite the pain, sometimes she even felt good. Not because of old memories but, strangely, because of the present.

This little stranger sometimes came up to her, took her hand, fussed with the shutters, heated water. The primus glowed with a blue fire and the girl's hands tucked the hot-water bottle (who had brought it and when?) under the red blanket.

Sometimes the doctor would come, inject Anastasia Georgievna with a tranquilizer, and when he left she would doze off, and then, late at night, the girl would doze off, too, not on the chairs now but on the floor, because the chairs "creaked badly."

When they needed money, Anastasia Georgievna got her reddish traveling bag out from under her pillow and paid, and she also gave the girl a little money. The girl didn't know whether this mysterious reserve of money would end one day or not, and if it did, then what was she going to do with the skinny, ill, and very tall Anastasia Georgievna?

One night Anastasia Georgievna woke up after a shot and felt the time had come for her to have a talk with the girl. She saw the room around her, the mantel with the flowerpot in the half-dark, the table with the portrait in the fanciful frame, and her mannish coat hanging on the nail by the door. In the still of the night she heard horses' hoofs clip-clopping and the wheels of heavy carts—at night here in Billancourt, sometimes, gilders arrange races to see who can outrun whom. It was hot in the room. She had been dreading just this night for so long, but now she wasn't afraid. No one was there. . . . No, someone was.

"Are you asleep?" she said.

The girl jumped up.

"Come over here. I have something to say to you."

The girl came over.

"I'm worried."

"But why! You shouldn't be."

"I'm afraid of suffering in my final days, and of what will happen after. And I don't know if you'll stay here or go back to Tverdotrubov."

"Listen to me," said the girl. "I'm going to talk softly. Don't worry about me, I'll stay at the Caprice, I'll go to work for Madame Klava. There's a Madame Klava here, have you heard of her?"

"No."

"That's too bad! She's a dressmaker. She's been asking me to come for a long time. So you see, I'm all set. You shouldn't be afraid of suffering, either. They'll give you a shot, we're not in the country. And what happens after—you can cut off my finger if it isn't all nonsense."

"What nonsense, what are you saying!"

"Exactly what I said. I saw when mama died. I washed the floor, and that was it."

Anastasia Georgievna took the girl's hand in both of hers.

"I'm still afraid you'll get scared of me and leave me alone. You're young."

"Nothing of the kind. I can do everything. Tverdotrubov was gone from morning on by then, he wasn't going to do it! I cleaned everything up, ran to the police station and the funeral office and haggled."

"Will you be able to close my eyes?"

"A great hardship!"

Anastasia Georgievna released the girl's hands and rested from their conversation a little.

"Now put your hand between the mattress and the feather-erbed. Even deeper. Do you feel it? Leave it for now. When I die, take it out and hide it. It's for you."

The girl pulled out her hand.

Anastasia Georgievna suddenly felt like drinking some thin sweet tea. The girl boiled the water and, without turning on the light, made tea and poured some for each of them. In the darkness they quietly drank their cups and spoke no more of this. But in the thick gray sky bright smudges appeared. It was after five.

When Anastasia Georgievna died (in the middle of the night, in bad weather), the girl immediately got out the fifty-three ten-ruble gold pieces from the *boudoir* days that were sewn into a velvet pouch and put two of them on Anastasia Georgievna's eyes, so that she could use them one last time. (Judging from her old skirts, Anastasia Georgievna had been accustomed to a different life, an unimaginable life.) Once she had done this, the little stranger turned to the rest: the jaw, the hands, the dressing, the owner of the Hotel Caprice, Billancourt City Hall, and the Russian church (one of the "forty forties").

When we learned this entire story in detail, many of us said out loud that Anastasia Georgievna Seyantseva had been lucky in Billancourt, no doubt about it.

1930

Versts and Sleeping Cars

My roads have not been easy roads, my roads have been largely rails. My young life jolted along the train tracks, but a canary is more important than I am. My roads led me from small towns to big cities, from forests to rivers and from cannons to billiard cues. This system of transport had its own minister—the Lord God, shall we say, only I've never seen him. There was doubtless some chief of locomotion, if only I could have had a glimpse of him. As a result of this locomotion, for a long time my feet itched and my soul tended to drift off. I recovered from this condition only very recently, all of four months ago.

We're not going to discuss the reasons for our journeys. We'll refrain. Our papers write about them every day. The reasons are always the same—here one minute, gone the next. An Englishman or Englishwoman might choose a good time for a little trip and take in a couple of thousand versts around Europe easy as pie, but we're not like that. After the first thousand we lose our equilibrium and then live the rest of our lives as beaten men.

Occasionally, too, an unhealthy condition besets us after all those journeys: you start thinking the journeys will never end, that you're still moving even when you're sitting in place, that the wheels are turning underneath you again, the telegraph poles are racing past, that it's carrying you, just count the turns. That's how it was with me, and it went on for a long time, but now it's over. Here's the station.

A woman was to blame for these protracted sensations, that is, of course, a young woman. What was she like? they ask. Large or small, what height approximately, and what coloring? We just can't seem to get along without asking those questions.

The questions are legitimate and basic. To this day people can't decide which is better, a large woman or a small one. They have reached no consensus on this point. The matter can even go as far as fisticuffs, son can rise up against father. Some get too worked up even to discuss the subject.

In my opinion, a small woman is a hundred, if not a hundred million times better than a large one. What can you do? You never know what side to embrace a large woman from. Before you can get your arms around her the whole process might even strike you as absurd. A large woman will never ask for anything and then will demand something impossible. A small women will simply say:

"Grigory Andreevich"—or "Grisha," or "Grishenka"—and you'll know she needs your protection or has a surprise for you.

Actually, it's been a long time since anyone called me Grishenka.

A small woman's foot, for instance, will fit entirely in your hand. Because she's small, you can look at a small woman from above and see the nicest part of her: the way she does her hair, her eyelashes, and the very tip of her nose. You have to look at a large woman from below and sometimes you simply never see anything past the cheeks; you have to guess about a lot from the expression of those cheeks, which are also large, naturally. And the objects a small woman finds need for are incomparably more appetizing: her gloves, or suit, even her handkerchief. . . . And it's true that there is much less litter from a small woman.

Actually, in Billancourt we have neither small nor large women. That is, we have both, but very few of either. This was particularly striking at Easter last year, when a full thousand men gathered at and around the church, and for this brave thousand—bathed, hair pomaded, polite and exchanging triple kisses—there were fewer than thirty women. A woman doesn't live in Billancourt, she flees to Paris.

In Paris both small and large women are in clover. In Paris there are handsome positions galore. For the most part, it's foreigners living there, in the evening the streets are lit up, and all the cabarets are full of cheerful, sober people, whereas here sometimes there's not even anywhere to sit on the Place Nationale—all the benches are taken. And then the men stand on the corners, pretending they're having a good time anyway. But the wind blows up their sleeves.

We don't have any women. What I mean to say is that we don't have nearly enough. And you can count the young women on your fingers. As embarrassing as it is to say, we have no prospective brides.

Not long ago we did have one who was as bright as a star in the sky. She was on the short side, she had even teeth, and she flashed her big blue eyes, her beautiful big blue eyes, all around. This was my fiancée.

It might sound funny, but I'd never had a fiancée before her. In Billancourt I hadn't had a chance to get myself a fiancée. When they sawed my clavicle in Rostov I proposed to one nurse, but I never saw her after that, and she and I lost touch. I wanted to look for her later, to apologize for my passionate raving, but I never did.

My journeys began at Zet junction. In those days, trains did not run on schedules. Our echelon had been transferred from the western line and was parked directly opposite the water pump, and from morning til night we hung around this water pump, or ran down the embankment, making the Plymouth Rock that roosted with the other hens on the station palisade swoon. One particularly nasty evening, we wrung the neck of this tempting Plymouth Rock and from it made such a soup that its owner, the junction chief, came by weeping with trembling knees, to taste the soup, and even thanked us, and when we offered him the neck, in view of his advanced age, he refused with tears in his eyes.

In the morning, though, there wasn't even half a spoonful left of the soup, so we took a walk through the nearby streets. No matter where you looked, the sky touched the earth. It was a mournful autumn, and late rooks soared in the sky—there was such a bird. The buildings for the most part looked uninhabited: the closed windows and flayed acacias seemed always to have been that way. Most of the shops were wrecked and nailed shut—not much in the way of shops to begin with. You would never find shops like that in Billancourt, let alone Paris. Nonetheless, somewhere we got a hold of a loaf of bread made from real sifted flour, some tobacco, stamps, and a gray, slightly sour tea they called "Ceylonsky." If I were to come across that

Ceylonsky, the manufacturer, now, I'd give him a good sock in the head.

As we were walking down the street, we saw a woman in a window, that is, a young woman. She was sitting there, sewing, as if it were nothing out of the ordinary. When a woman sits in the window and sews, well, it's like a picture in a frame.

"Won't you give us something to drink, mademoiselle? Don't be afraid, we're not expecting anything alcoholic!" We called to her through the window, tapped on the glass with our fingers, and bowed. Me and my buddy.

She opened the window partway and frowned. It was autumn 1919, and there was a wind up.

"You'd better come through the front door," she said, "or the room will get chilly."

The window closed and we walked around to the front door.

Heels clicked down steps, and the old door yielded with a rusty creak.

"Mademoiselle," my buddy said, "please keep your distance. We may already have typhus."

"That's all right," she said. "*Merci.*"

She brought us an earthenware pitcher of milk, a pitcher as pink as the sky. She was wearing a thimble on her finger; there are women who are adorned just as well with a thimble as a ring.

"What are they saying, though, will you be leaving soon?" she asked shyly, and she twisted her foot in its patent shoe.

"We don't have the right to talk about that."

"You don't have to. I know myself you're leaving."

"As you like."

"But where are your horses?"

"We're infantry."

"I'm going to give you something for good luck."

My buddy stuck out his hand.

Without thinking, she removed the thimble from her skinny, not perfectly straight finger and put it in my buddy's open hand.

"That's all," she said, and clutching the empty pitcher to her chest, she went up the stairs. It would have been pointless to ask her to stay.

When I returned to Zet junction a month later, that building was nowhere to be found. At least five blocks had burned to the ground, and the neighborhood's inhabitants were dreaming of planting potatoes in those places. But I had actually come to return the thimble: my buddy didn't need it anymore, they'd buried my buddy. Rest in peace, Kolya.

So the wheels jolted along beneath me, the telegraph wire flashed by in the sky, barring the way for all the rooks, the waves roared by the feed crops on the Crimean shores, and I was racing along at top speed. The sea wasn't just the sea, the sea was the one we had sailed under the tsars, from the Varangians to the Greeks.

In the upper left-hand pocket of my tunic the thimble, like a jewel, like some kind of pearl, was racing with me to a far-off land. Anyone else in my place would have tossed it onto the waves of the Bosporus long before or buried it in the Turkish earth. After all, not only did I have no use for it—it wouldn't go on my pinky—but it had brought my buddy irrevocable harm. I wouldn't think about it for weeks on end—once or twice I shook it out the window while cleaning Balkan dirt off my tunic, and once I lost it in a move in the folds of my suitcase (the suitcase lining swallowed up a number of tiny objects at that time). But the thimble always returned to me, never letting me forget that voice, those eyes, and those dear shoes.

Truth be told, I didn't try to forget them. What was there for me to remember if not them? Nothing, I guess. I recalled the building, the window, the acacia, as if it were all still there, as if it had not been swept whole into the beyond, along with its curtains and door knobs, by a heartless, well-aimed shell. It was as if this dear building had not been borne away with all its jambs and lintels to a heavenly valley but was living out its peaceful days on a quiet street with a marvelous woman—a young woman, that is—in the window.

And the farther I went, the more my soul sought that framed picture I had once glimpsed. My heart ached in the Saros Gulf, in Tyrnov I didn't sleep one night in three, in Rudnik I started discussing whether it wouldn't be natural for this picture to turn up again in my distant journeying. But when I moved to Prague—I don't mean to boast, I was in Prague, too—I began paying more attention to the female staff at the Russian cafeteria. Hope overwhelmed me.

At that time, I was in my sixth year of traveling with no end in sight. And then, in Prague, I saw her.

"Hello," I said. "I have the honor of having met you during the civil war, which was so hard for each and every one of us."

"Excuse me," she said, "but I don't know you."

"Excuse me," I said, "but you do know me: here's your thimble."

And right there on the stairs I pulled out the slightly dented but perfectly fine thimble.

"I'm sorry," she said again, "but I didn't lose a thimble."

I wouldn't let her go, though. On the contrary, I took a step closer. I was ready to take her by the hand, but it didn't go that far. Since the time she had clutched the pitcher of milk to her chest she had curled her hair and bought herself a new dress.

The people who used the Russian cafeteria were not altogether poor, not entirely down and out, so to speak.

"Do you know there's not a trace left of your building or the neighboring buildings, if I may say so?"

"What building? You must be confused. Such a strange man you are."

I took a step closer to her. She came up to my shoulder. Her eyes were the same.

"There's a famous American war picture playing at the cinema," I said. "Would you go with me?"

"Why not? *Merci.*"

In Prague, going into the fog is like going out in a smoking field. The thought of losing her frightened me. I took her arm in mine and leaned toward her to swallow a little of her air. When we walked under the streetlamps, I could see every single hair, every freckle, and since there could be nothing nicer than this, I kept trying to break out of the fog under the streetlamps, pulling her to the left, then the right, and back, gazing into her face.

By the time the American war picture was over it was nighttime.

"I'm leaving tomorrow," she said.

"Where are you going?"

"Paris."

She led me down a dark lane. She'd managed to get used to me a little and even laughed occasionally. I listened to her and saw a long road, my road to Paris, which was steep and scary and took my breath away.

"This is where I live," she said suddenly.

How had she been able to find the right building in this gloom?

"So, will you take the thimble?" I asked warily. "Or shall I bring it to Paris?"

"Such a strange man you are," she repeated and smiled, and then suddenly she became sad, and still sad, she went into the building.

I walked away from the door and remembered the address—#45. This night might have had a terrible effect on the nerves of someone less tough than I am. I was fine, though. I was happy.

Paris is not Prague. It might as well be a month's journey from Prague to Paris—so different are the cities. Over Paris, the sky splits open and a dove flies from the clouds; the sun over Paris is a white sun. And if it's raining lightly, it's as if people had begun dancing in the streets: the men (have you noticed?) walk through the puddles on tiptoe, and the women dash across the street and immediately lift a foot to see whether their stocking was splashed—Oh yes, it was!—and run on.

This is Paris. And Billancourt is next door.

I arrived in winter, one morning, very early, the same morning snow fell briefly. I hadn't been able to leave Prague right away. A year had passed, a long and difficult year. I arrived in the morning, left my things with a buddy, cleaned myself up, and went out. I was looking for a street and address. I started wandering in the vicinity, as if I were taking in the city.

That entire long year I had been thinking about this building, imagining it. Lots of people lived in it besides Taniusha, lots of men and women, large and small. And one of them (a small one, naturally) still seemed to me like the end point of my wanderings. My versts and sleeping cars!

After I had examined everything she came out, alone, and I barred her way, stretching my arms out so she couldn't get by. She wanted to pass under my arm but halted, staring at me full in the face and then she recognized me.

"You've become quite the beautiful lady!" I exclaimed. And it was true, her eyelashes were like spider's legs, and her gloves were kid.

"I recognize you," she said, and gave me her hand.

"Do you remember the American war picture?"

But she didn't.

"Your address was #45."

"Is that really important?"

I couldn't tell what she was thinking at that moment.

She started walking with me and telling me that her father was in America and she was planning to go visit him. She was going to bring money back to get married.

"To whom?"

"I'll be back soon, by spring."

So I went to America. . . . That is, naturally not. I stayed here, though I might as well have gone there, in her wake. But Monsieur Renault—that's another story, which doesn't concern us now. I went to see him through the passage that lets out on the embankment, where they interview and hire people—and where, by the way, they toss them out on their ears. In short, I hurried after her, but lagged behind.

Oh, America, the ocean! My native land!

In the evenings I would walk the Billancourt streets (don't laugh: the Paris stars burn over Billancourt at night!) and think about the fact that it was probably broad daylight in America now. I saw its green steppes, its sandpipers, its cherry orchards, and all its natural charms: broad rivers like ours, thick forests, nameless roads. That's how I viewed America at the time.

I thought about myself, about the fact that my life kept moving down the highways, that my friends had come to a stop long before but I was still going. And about the fact that my friend and I were breathing soot, and we were hot from the open-hearth furnaces, and despite the fact that I had moved into a room I got from my bosses, the verst markers kept racing up to me.

It blows hard up our sleeves, anyone can tell you that. It takes a few shots of our native spirit—less than that won't make it right. It's medicine, not alcohol. At night you get a little feverish once or twice but no more. We have short nights. If you have a fever, the best thing is to shut the door tight to deter visitors and turn your face to the wall.

And now there was a knock at the door. I opened the door with my left hand and switched on the light with my right.

"Excuse me," someone said on the other side of the door. "I guess you were sleeping. I've been here with friends, the Petrovs," (or maybe it was the Vedrovs) "and learned you were living here so I decided to look you up."

"From America?"

"Yes."

I closed the door, pulled up my trousers, put on my jacket, turned up my collar, and fastened the snap at my neck with my finger.

She sat down on the chair and looked around. She was in my room, she had come to see me. She needed me.

"Well, how are things going on the western front, no changes?"

"None whatsoever."

"Did you get settled?"

"Yes, I did."

She now had a gold tooth and her hair had been dyed a strange color.

"I waited for you to come to America. But you didn't."

I actually got upset.

"Don't joke with me, Taniusha. I'm still very delicate inside."

She put her foot on the heating pipe.

"I'm not joking. I kept thinking, what if he keeps his word? But you didn't."

"You mean I should chase you all over the world? Don't distances mean anything to a young girl?"

"Why have you started talking in verse?" she said in an unfriendly way. "Since when did you become a poet?"

There was a moment of silence.

"I can't keep chasing after you everywhere. As it is, I see no end to my journeys. My entire life is nothing but versts and sleeping cars."

"What sleeping cars? You mean the ones that go cross-wise?"

"The very same." She looked out the window. But I didn't take my eyes off her. I had come to the preliminary conclusion that I didn't recognize her.

Yet it was she. She seemed to be searching for something

else to say but not finding it. And I couldn't help her there.

"Well then, I'll be going. I see you don't have any news for me. But I have lots."

That scared me.

"I didn't bring back any money, and I didn't get married. It's like news on the telegraph. I don't know where to start. I'll tell you another time."

My head started spinning, I didn't know what I was saying, and I kept my finger on my snap.

"Marry me. You've been my fiancée for a long time. We'll go to Harbin together. Or Nice."

"Why Harbin?"

"A little while ago someone from back home left for Harbin, he says it's better there."

She looked at me with dismay and began tying her scarf.

"Your fiancée. . . . What, do you consider a thimble an engagement ring? It wasn't even given to you."

We both stood up simultaneously, and because she was a very small woman, she passed under my arm.

I was left standing there, paralyzed, as if my train had come to a sudden halt and I had fallen from the upper berth onto my neighbor and my suitcase had fallen on us both from the upper berth. Her steps died away. I looked to see whether she had forgotten anything because then I would have run after her.

People know me in Billancourt. I have a long road behind me, no one here has such a long road. But now it's quiet all around, like in the sky.

1930

The Billancourt Manuscript

Vania Lyokhin died on Tuesday night, the 7th, in the thirty-sixth year of his hard but colorful life.

"Drop your bachelor doings," Shchov said to me. "Vania Lyokhin's dead."

I dropped my bachelor doings and left. I didn't have far to go: Vania Lyokhin lived in the Hotel Caprice, but how he lived—there's no point getting into that.

As I entered I suddenly didn't want to look. I wanted to cough and say, "All right, Vania Lyokhin, get up. It's no good lying around, you're no fine lady!" But I didn't, I stared at Vania's ashen face, walked around the bed, and sat down at the table. His will lay on the table. Shchov had just pulled it out of a drawer. It concerned him and me.

One other person was mentioned in it as well, but it's not a name for the press. The daughter of the Hotel Caprice's owner was fully accounted for in it. We didn't have to go far to find her: she was standing at the head of the bed, blowing her nose, eyebrows raised, and crying. That morning she'd shaved Vania with her own hands. He hadn't finished drinking the lemonade she'd squeezed for him before dinner. She used all these mundane details to keep Vania's soul from slipping away, but it didn't work, his soul was already gone.

Across the street, in the dappled twilight, a priest was walking along with a briefcase under his arm, his cassock swinging back and forth. I stood up and put the will back on the table.

"What's wrong with you?" said Shchov. "You should read it. There are some curious things in it, you know."

I knew Vania Lyokhin could not possibly have left millions. He wasn't that kind of person. And I felt sorry for him.

"I'll get to it," I told Shchov. "I'm going downstairs. I'll meet the priest."

Thirty-five years of life is nothing to sneeze at. It's as if the hands of the clock said it was four o'clock, as if the page on the calendar from Wednesday to Thursday had been torn off, that's what thirty-five years is. The very middle of a day, a week, a life; time surges behind and in front of you, like water.

A couple of days later Vania Lyokhin was carried through his own Billancourt streets. The heavily burdened, not terribly frisky mare, wearing blinkers as big as skillets, stepped out. The coachman gathered up the reins, tch'ked at the horse, and yawned right and left. Vania Lyokhin was half covered with a white rug or some other sturdy stuff, and just behind the rail, looking at Vania Lyokhin right through the wheels, Shchov and I walked with our other friends, the infantrymen and workmen; a sympathetic French crowd we didn't know very well came along with us; and even the daughter of the Hotel Caprice's owner, a very sweet-faced young woman, walked with us, sobbing.

They carried him down a familiar street past Mr. Salmson's tedious buildings and fences, where all of us have done and will do our share of walking. They carried Vania Lyokhin past the very streetlamp where not that long ago our army-mate cracked up in a car while in a drunken stupor, past those gates where for a year a single Russian word had been written in coal—everyone knows it. They brought Vania Lyokhin to our new cemetery, where no matter how many flowers you ask for no one puts any, where the weather in winter is raw and in summer dusty and where—like it or not—you and I, too, will be buried not far from Vania Lyokhin.

They carried Vania past rusty, useless black wreaths to a deep hole. Naturally they didn't bury him where there are promenades, statues, and flowers. They buried him in section five, where he would lie peacefully for five years next to Gustopsov, Semenchuk, and Dementiev, where you could see a smokestack very close by, our smokestack, a famous smokestack, actually. A piece of mirror had been glued to a wire decoration and on it was a gold leaf portrait of a Chinese youth, U Yu Men, who also of course had had nothing and so was buried here.

For five minutes the priest painted a picture of Vania Lyokhin's life. An airplane buzzed overhead; I don't know whether anyone up there noticed us as we shifted from foot to foot around the grave. Vania Lyokhin had a modest mound built up over him out of earth, sand, and stones, and a short cross was planted with an inscription of who lay there and when he died. We might have liked to depict many other things on this cross, but there wasn't room. In the other sections, where the promenades and flowers were, the tombstones had room for entire histories.

The tall cart with the folded white rug clattered off on its way back, though at first the mare had not seemed terribly frisky. That means the mare was faking when she was pulling Vania Lyokhin. And once again I felt sorry for him. But Shchov said: "Turn right around and go straight to the Hotel Caprice. You have to see the will."

I turned my collar up and followed Shchov. We got well ahead of the others (no more than ten of them) and the young lady—so sweet, really, and still so very young. People say they adored one another, like husband and wife.

The will really did prove to contain some surprising points. Who would ever have thought anything of the kind about Vania Lyokhin? As I had expected, he did not leave millions. He gave his linen and clothing to Shchov, his boots to the poor, and asked that his automatic pen, tie, and tobacco pouch (from *those* days) be left for a museum of Billancourt life, should one ever come to be. Vania instructed that all the small stuff—his hairbrush, three postcards, a piece of something unidentifiable, a French grammar book, and a family photograph—be given to the daughter of the Hotel Caprice's owner, and to me he designated a manuscript in a file held together with an old rubber band. It was this that amazed both Shchov and me: our Vania Lyokhin, it turned out, had been planning to become a Russian writer, another Mamin-Sibiryak, in fact!

It was dusk. Across the street, at the Cabaret, a gramophone started playing. People were walking by outside. Women were picking up a few items—not mothers of families, though, not wives, not housewives. *They* go out in the morning, they take their children to school at a regular time, they do everything on a schedule. No, these were the dolls from the street that's right by the river, that crosses ours, dolls who had just arisen, who had bright yellow hair, raucous voices, haunches draped in black silk, and legs like upside-down seltzer bottles. But even dolls like to eat—meat, cheese, a bottle of red wine—so they go out for food at dusk, and they walk, and they curse, and they linger listening to "Stenka Razin" on the Cabaret gramophone, and they stop to examine the perfume and pomade on display in the window of Boris Gavrilovich's hairdressing salon. And then they go back down that cross-street where at night there's music, and shooting, and drunken shouting in eight languages.

I opened the old file in my room, under the lamp. Inside that file was the breath of Vania Lyokhin, breath from his never-once-pierced chest. The manuscript was long, about a hundred pages. To all appearances, this was only the beginning of some-thing—a novel, shall we say. He had made a fair copy of the first twenty pages in the most earnest way, but the rest were still messy—I'm certain Vania Lyokhin would never have shown the last pages to the woman he adored. The paper the novel was written on was marked off in squares, and the handwriting was the Vanialyokhin-ish handwriting I knew so well, slanting down, with loops.

From my first glance a question crept into my soul: Was the novel the cause of his death, dear Vania Lyokhin's death? All of a sudden I realized that something had burned inside him as if it were on fire, and it was because of this long-burning fire that he couldn't go on living. How come we never guessed the agony his imagination was causing him? This could be happening to some other friend, too, without us ever knowing! But none of our friends would ever admit it. Myself first of all.

I began to read the writing he had bequeathed me.

◆ ◆ ◆

The night was black. The last leaves were blowing off the trees. When I walked away from the station you could still discern the smoke escaping from the chimney, the flickering in the window, and the green fire by the station house. Then the gloom moved in. The ruts of the road, washed by the rains, were just now dark, and my foot kept landing in them. The clouds were racing by.

I walked for quite a while. The field came to an end, and so did the woods. Once, a very long time ago, two sides first had fought in these woods, then they had killed and looted. The road went uphill. At an exposed spot the wind nearly knocked me off my feet. A cemetery stretched out. I imagined returning here tomorrow morning, in the gray weather, and recognizing the straight path, the lilac bushes, the stone on my father's grave.

The municipal hospital partly blocked my view. The town began.

I knew this town. I knew these streets. Trees swayed inside palisades, dripped rain, creaked. In the town, though, it was quieter. From time to time a gate would bust open and from the depths of the yard a dog would hurl itself at me in silence and then immediately stand back. I did not encounter another soul at that late hour. I counted the crossings and made the turns from memory. At one corner I came across a half-torn-down sign: Karl Liebnecht Street. I thought I recognized the intersection. It used to be Ekaterinskaya.

A few hundred steps from the spot where I was now walking, I knew, paved streets began, maybe there was even a beer stand still open, lights on in the building, a lamp behind the colored curtain, or a late trolley passing. But I couldn't hear anything because of the wind. And I walked on, the way blind men walk through their own houses.

At last, I found my building, I saw the address, the same one I had been putting on envelopes for so many years. Two steps led to the porch. The windows were dark. But above the roof, above the old chimney, the clouds were moving.

The windows were shuttered from the inside— that was the custom in my town.

There wasn't any bell. You had to knock, but knocking in the night might frighten them. I listened carefully for something stirring in the house, but at that hour probably only I was awake in the whole town.

I put my ear to the door and knocked twice. Something slammed somewhere, maybe three blocks away. Someone scuffling felt slippers came up to the door. I grabbed the doorpost and squeezed my suitcase handle with my other hand. I could feel my heart knocking in my chest. In the darkness, an unseen hand touched the lock.

"Who's there?' asked a quiet male voice suddenly close to me.

"Vania Lyokhin," I answered just as quietly.

The handle turned. The door opened. An eye beamed at me, big, black, and shining.

"Come in,' said the man. 'This is quite an event! Only quietly, no need to wake them. It's night, let them sleep. They're tired during the day."

My suitcase and I squeezed through the door. Now, in the gloom, I couldn't see anything. Somewhere a clock was ticking calmly and fairly loudly.

"I should introduce myself," said the man in a whisper, and I sensed him extending his hand toward me. "Moisei Borisovich Gotovy, Sonia's husband."

I took his hand, which was small and burning.

"Follow me," he whispered again. "I'll show you our kitchen."

He took me by the hand. According to my memories there ought to have been a staircase here to the second floor, but there wasn't. A door opened without a sound, and we moved silently, as if we were sailing. We went in where it was warmer and the air was different.

A match was struck and a shadow passed across a burner and some shelves. I saw a small man leaning over a lamp. The smell of warm kerosene reached me; the flame jumped briefly in the glass.

"Sit down," said Moisei Borisovich. "Now you'll get some fish soup. Today we had fish soup for dinner."

"What about Sonia?" I asked quietly.

"Sit down, I'll tell you. Sonia is dreaming. Why didn't you warn us? The surprise could make someone ill."

"And mama?"

"Your mama will be back tomorrow morning. She went to see relatives."

"What relatives? What for?"

"Shh! What are you shouting so for? There are children here."

He fished a piece of perch and a long thin carrot out of the kettle. He sliced off a piece of bread, hugging the loaf to his chest. Now I got a good look at this man: he was over forty and he was wearing long drawers and a shirt. Light black hairs stuck up from the top of his head, and the same little hairs poked out of his large ears and even the nostrils of his heavy nose. He sat down opposite me and our gazes met. We looked at each other for a long time.

"Well, eat your soup," he said, agitated. "This is quite an event!"

He lowered his eyes.

I ate the perch and bread. And the bread seemed alive to me, it breathed, it saw me, it reached out for me, entered into me, satiated me and made me happy.

"It's so quiet here," I said. "Everywhere."

"Yes, now, thank God. . ." he replied, and a half-forgotten fright flashed in his moist eyes.

I finished eating.

"I know one interesting thing," he said suddenly. "I'll put you in mama's room, we don't have another bed, we have two other rooms. People live upstairs."

I didn't reply.

"Only quietly, you mustn't make any noise. Take your baggage." I picked up the suitcase. "We'll go through the bedroom. But then how you'll sleep! Just like in Paris."

He blew out the lamp. We were left in total darkness, and he again took me by the hand and led me. We
sailed. A door opened, then another. I lost my orienta-
tion and walked as if in a dream. The darkness, the
uncertainty, and the black night were making my head
spin. I held his small, hot hand and felt each joint of his
hairy fingers. Then his hand slipped out of mine. The
light blazed on.

With the ceiling light on, I recognized the room
I'd been born in.

Above the bed, above the dark featherbed, hung a
portrait of my father, lackluster and not at all like him.
There was my own portrait from the '16 draft, and on
the table, like a warm house pet, lay her knitting with
her needles sticking into it.

Moisei Borisovich looked at me, and there was
curiosity in his big eyes. Then he nodded to me,
hitched up his drawers, exposing his skinny, hairy
ankles, and disappeared behind the door. And no matter how hard I listened, I heard nothing more.

I took off my boots and slowly circled the room,
and everything, from the rug that yielded under my
feet to the round mirror (which had seemed so high
when I was a child), everything suddenly became mine
again. In these old, dusty, and perhaps even worm-
eaten things, my soul met the souls of the people who
lived here. Weary, I sat down on the bed and lingered
for an hour and a half with the vague thoughts that
were running through my mind. It wasn't any one of
them that held my memory in thrall, except maybe, on

its own track, the thought of Madeleine's letter. I had promised to write immediately. There could be no question of that. But some phrases for the coming day did pop up and ready themselves in my mind:

"I only just arrived. The train was late. There were a million people. I searched for the house in awful weather in a totally dead town. Of course, I was worried, like an idiot. My sister's husband greeted me, *un type assez rigolo*. Sonia and the children were sleeping, and mama's coming back tomorrow. I'll write you more, I can imagine what it would cost you to come here. . . . How is everything with you? Are you well? Write about everything. Did you get my postcard from Moscow? Whom have you seen of our dear friends? What's going on at the Caprice? Send regards to everyone, especially Shchov, and thank him for the cheese he slipped me without anyone noticing as I was leaving. . . ."

I put a stop to the flow, finally. I stretched out on the featherbed without undressing. The ceiling light was still on when I fell asleep. The wind howled in the chimney of the big tile stove.

When I awoke it was daytime, there were noise and light, the shutters were open and things were happening in the next room. I sat up in bed and immediately the door opened very quietly and I saw four child's eyes.

The two were perfectly identical, about six or seven. Their hands hung straight at their sides, they didn't blink, they didn't close their mouths. Their pants were laundered, their little jackets mended. I beckoned them to me and kissed each one on the head. They smelled of feathers.

"I have an orange," I told them, and I opened my suitcase.

They had never seen an orange, and they poked their thin, sharp-nailed fingers into it. I gave them a chocolate bar and the empty cheese box with the laughing cow on the lid, and I held their cold, fragile hands in mine.

"Do you know who I am?"

Yes, they knew.

"Hurry up, then, tell your mama to come in."

I stood up and Sonia ran into the room.

She came in with a painfully tense face, as happens when people are trying at all costs to keep from giving away what they're feeling. She was wearing an old fall coat instead of a bathrobe. I hugged her and felt how terribly, how unrecognizably fat she'd become, how low and heavy her breasts hung, how stooped her shoulders were.

She couldn't say a word. Tears streamed down her face, and I found myself thinking what a stranger she had become to me, she who had once bathed in the same tub with me. Her hands, which I remembered as the light hands of a schoolgirl, were large and stiff, and she wore her heavy engagement ring on her pinky now. There was something halfway between timidity and envy in her eyes as she stared at me.

"You, you," she repeated. "Look what you've become! A Frenchman! A White Guard! Ah!" She started crying. "Many of your kind have come back this last year, but did we really believe it? Take care you don't kill mama!"

She and I were standing by the window, and I noticed I was almost not looking at her anymore, I was looking out the window. Looking out the window at the quiet gray street.

A man there was pushing a hand cart, and the house across the way had the most *ordinary* look. It was a private house, only the windows had been shattered and the porch was littered with fallen leaves. And at a certain instant that had probably been fixed a thousand years before that day, coming around the corner, I saw *her.*

She had the kind of walk that people do in their seventh decade, people who have become one with the land, their arms held slightly away from their bodies, with a slight spring in their knees. She had become small and probably very light; she was wearing a rather wide skirt down to her heels and a thick woolen fitted jacket. On her head was a tan woolen kerchief that outlined a knot of what was now probably all gray hair. She was carrying a homemade cloth purse and a long, needle-thin umbrella with a white handle. She crossed the street near our porch and walked up the steps.

Through the open doors, through the room where Moisei Borisovich was helping his sons, I saw the door open in the vestibule, I saw her walk in and carefully shut and lock the door, I saw her wipe her feet on the doormat and unhurriedly begin to shake out her kerchief. And then I stepped toward her.

At that same instant she turned around. I thought she would cry out, fall down, and I hurried, my arms outstretched, to catch her. But she seemed to detach herself from the floor and float toward me. . . .

◆ ◆ ◆

And so on and so forth.

There were about a hundred pages, as I already said, but now it was all clear to me: Vania Lyokhin had died of imagination. It had turned into a fever that must have been ripping him apart this entire last year, but what a wonderful man! Billancourt loses out on every score. Its best people die; the decent ones pass away. They abandon themselves, secretly at first, to all kinds of gloomy distractions and torture themselves each according to his abilities. But some don't have far to go. They pick up a pen and paper and start writing. And it's a sad sight: that kind of energy doesn't befit them, that kind of energy will consume them twice over.

Thus we shall remain, my friends, infantry and workmen, what we have always been! We don't need a pen, or paper, or an inkwell. We won't let fame, or large sums of money, or the love of a bewitching creature disturb our dreams. Keep your head down, advises a guy experienced in these matters.

Let other people write about us. We ourselves—whatever we imagine—we aren't writers!

1930

Ring of Love

Roman Germanovich, who had a Teutonic last name as well, and his wife, née Bychkova, climbed the stairs, caught their breath, looked around, and rang the doorbell. Roman Germanovich was old and dry, and he made a rustling sound as he moved. Née-Bychkova looked like a real gypsy: dark, heavy brows, thick lips, and a little mustache and chin whiskers to go with her handsome black eyes. She wore a locket on her broad chest, a silver bracelet on her arm, and a sapphire ring on her finger. Her skirts of rustling silk covered swollen legs, which ached from the stairs, and her hat was constantly at odds with her steep knot of black hair, into which she had stuck a carved comb with diamonds for going calling.

"Roman Germanovich," said née-Bychkova, "your suit is twisted."

Roman Germanovich put himself in order with a light rustle and gave his spouse a grateful look.

It was Sunday, a hot and dusty Sunday, with closed shutters, howling gramophones, and pomaded hair. In that kind of heat, as in a time of cholera, Billancourt expires, the sparrows flock to the river, and there is no sky as such. It's not light or dark blue; it's the color of glass. The air doesn't move and someone sleeps crosswise on the burning hot sidewalk, in the accidental shade of a chestnut that lost its blossoms in the last storm. In that kind of heat, as in a time of cholera, people don't go calling, but this had been decided back in April. . . . *What* had been decided?

Née-Bychkova had been living in a state of agitation since April. True, she had lived her entire life in a state of agitation. That was her temperament. And this despite the fact that she loved her husband well, and they even had a son, a young man just this side of grown. Née-Bychkova had her own memories from before her marriage, memories of flowers so vivid they would not leave her in peace, and the more they wouldn't the more certain she became that her life could not end this way, that some final trumpet had yet to blow one final note. Before April such thoughts often tore at her, but in April she learned precisely how this story could end and she began preparing for it.

It was then that she met Murochka and Murochka. She-Murochka was expecting a son (she would hear nothing of a daughter) and he-Murochka still dreamed of a daughter and had even thought up a name for her—Lida. Each of them was trying to win née-Bychkova over when out of the blue she asked in her stern, low, ringing voice: "I'm sorry, what is your last name? Did I hear right?"

"Kryatov," they told her.

"Might Vladimir Georgievich Kryatov be your relative?" And she twisted the sapphire ring on her fat finger.

He-Murochka cried out:

"Kingdom of heaven, he's my uncle! I mean, if he isn't dead. We ought to inquire. My uncle, my uncle! Did you know him?"

And she-Murochka said: "He lives in Serbia. He must be seventy at least."

"Sixty-nine," said née-Bychkova.

They started asking all the essential questions: When had she known Kryatov? Had she known him well? And where? And was it true that he had been a handsome young man?

She answered that it had all happened thirty years ago, she had known him very well, as well as anyone could, in Moscow, and he had indeed been a handsome man.

And right then and there, at this first acquaintance, she hurriedly opened the locket on her broad chest. Murochka and Murochka looked at it as if they were looking into née-Bychkova's very soul. There in the locket was the man himself, Vladimir Kryatov, complete with mustache and beard. The lid snapped shut.

Née-Bychkova also showed them her old gypsy bracelet, which he had admired in those days, and let them spin the sapphire ring, his last gift, on their fingers. It had been in the pawn shop three times in the last few years, but thank God she had managed to hold onto it, and now she would hold onto it forever because, also thank God, the dark days were over for her and Roman Germanovich, and their son would soon be a Frenchman and an engineer.

Murochka and Murochka did not know what to say. They turned the conversation to other people, to themselves, to their little boy or little girl. Née-Bychkova noticed this, closed her eyes, and said: "You're right to be surprised that I would tell you about myself and Vladimir Georgievich right away. But what's there to be ashamed of, and whatever for? There was a revolution and now we stand naked before one another. We have nothing to hide. Now we can say anything. What secrets could people have after the troubles we have seen? And so I ask you, find out, if you can, whether Vladimir Georgievich is dead or alive so that I can pray for him."

It was not like her to smile. She raised her eyebrows, her eyes glittered, she said simple things in a quiet voice, and she made very little noise, only the creak of her velvet shoes, because of her heavy gait, and the rustle of her silk dress.

"Still, he is our relative," said Murochka. "We should write to him at the old address. The old address in the yellow book."

A live Vladimir Georgievich Kryatov emerged from a yellow book in née-Bychkova's dreams.

In her heart it felt as if that final trumpet had started playing right by her side. Her life had in fact turned out to be not just any life but a real life. The memories of the vivid flowers, the hope, the terrible and sweet secrets in her soul, everything had combined into a single mounting happy force. She dreamed of Kryatov emerging from a yellow book and walking toward her. What should she say? Where should she look? During the day, despite the fact that she loved her husband well, all she could think about was Kryatov. Her entire life in Billancourt became transparent, and through it she could see their meeting.

Roman Germanovich rang again. A child—a little girl, naturally—was whining inside, and someone was pouring water and shouting for someone to open the front door.

Murochka opened it all the way. There was delight on his

face, and he began wiping his feet on the doormat. Née-
Bychkova went in first, said hello, took a lace handkerchief
(fragrant with perfume from the days of Max Linder and the
subduing of the Crimea) from her purse and wiped her damp
face. Murochka ran out with her belly, deflated, of course.

"He came!" she whispered in a concerned voice, not really
greeting née-Bychkova very kindly. "He came after the very
first letter, rushed here. And why? He thought we lived well.
Now he doesn't know where to go. He wants to find work as a
groom."

She led her guests into the dining room with the picture on
the wall and the lampshade in the middle.

At the table sat Kryatov, who had shaved his mustache and
beard. His mouth had been open for a smile, so he carefully
replaced his upper jaw on his lower. He was wearing a green,
single-breasted jacket and a shirt without a collar, and he looked
like a retired land captain who had galloped forty versts without changing horses or setting foot out of his carriage.

"Here, uncle, Roman Germanovich and his wife," said
Murochka. "I believe you know each other from the old days."

Kryatov began to get up without raising his eyes, reached
for née-Bychkova's hand, and said: "What do you mean, certainly, I have had the pleasure."

It was not like her to show her feelings in front of everyone.
She gave him her hand with the ring, which she had worn
(when it wasn't in hock) along with her engagement ring all her
life. He kissed her long satin sleeve and sat down without waiting to see where she would sit. It had been three days now and
he still hadn't recovered from his trip: so much money had been
spent on this journey, so many hopes laid on it!

The shutters in the dining room had been closed, so it was cool. In the corner was an oak sideboard, and on the table were white cups with a blue design—squiggles that looked like punctuation marks.

"It's hot today," said Roman Germanovich with a quiet rustle as he sat on the edge of a chair. He liked to talk about the weather. "They say in Petersburg it's hot, too, and the white nights are continuing. Allow me to remind you that the nights can be chilly. These white nights occur in the north in June and May. Such an interesting phenomenon."

Murochka poured him some tea.

"Foreigners can't understand the white nights," Roman Germanovich continued. "Even our son, a future engineer, can't. If I'm not mistaken, you're from Serbia. A fraternal Slavic country. But there probably aren't any white nights there, either."

"I was lately noticing," Kryatov replied, and he worked his mouth a little.

Finally he looked at the guests with the hostile eyes of an old man who could no longer see anything up close and had a tiresome way of looking into the distance at details no one cared about. He reached for a cookie.

Née-Bychkova sat across from him in her usual stillness. She smelled old fabric, camphor, and tobacco. This was not the pleasant smell of old age that Roman Germanovich, her spouse, had about him.

"And of course we had a little girl," Murochka was saying just then, rocking in her chair. "Wouldn't you like to see? The christening was on the fifth, and we named her Lidochka. Roman Germanovich, you simply must take a look."

"Happy to, happy to," rustled Roman Germanovich. "I'm

sure the conditions are sanitary. . . . If you please, at your service."

They led him to the doorway. Née-Bychkova made a movement but stayed seated. Kryatov took another cookie.

"What thoughtlessness, what idiotic thoughtlessness," he began, moving his jaw rhythmically and wiping his fingers on the tablecloth, "having children in our day and age, isn't it? People have nothing to eat and they're giving birth. They won't help out their old relatives who rocked them in their arms, they only know how to keep inflicting pain. Oh yes this, oh yes that, are you alive, do you remember us? Here's a chance to get out of this backwater, I thought, to know a little peace for whatever time I have left. I packed my things, borrowed from everybody, and set out. They're telling me to get a job as a groom: room and board, and even three hundred francs' pay being offered by some Bourbon with claims to the throne. And that's it."

She listened to the child's cry in the other room.

"Vladimir Georgievich, you must not recognize me."

She leaned toward him across the table. She smiled at him, showing a row of large, even, young teeth, which made her entire face look young.

He stared at her with his far-sighted, unfocused, faded blue eyes and leaned back in his chair to see her better, but said nothing.

She kept smiling.

"N-n-no, madame, forgive me. . . . How is it . . . ?"

But at that moment his glance fell on the plump gypsy hand and the sapphire ring.

"Aah! . . . Yes, yes . . . And so we meet! Only I don't recall your name."

"Varvara, Varia," said née-Bychkova.

Now he looked into her eyes. His chin trembled a little, and two glassy tears welled up in his eyes.

"Aha. . . . How nice. I'm stunned. That was a long time ago."

"Yes."

"You had a yellow shawl, I remember. Your apartment was near Petrovsky Park."

"You furnished that apartment for me."

"Yes, yes. . . A yellow shawl, like now. . . I remember."

She listened to the voices in the next room again.

"A cab, wintertime, the frost. That was fine. Life was thrilling then. Wasn't it? Ah, those Moscow experiences. . . ."

She looked at the door, she was very worried they might come in. Flies were circling the lampshade, dive-bombing it, swarming.

"So you're alone now, is that right? Widowed?"

"It's been twelve years now since she was buried. Diphtheria. She was a saint. I didn't think I'd survive. There's not another like her in the world. An angel!"

"Did you have children?"

"One son, a scoundrel if there ever was one, forgive me, yes. . . . I threw him out. Now I don't know where he is. They say he hanged people."

"Didn't you get a large dowry, though?"

"Yes, yes. Certain forests in Penza province, for logging. They stole it all."

She looked without blinking, listening.

"But didn't you have a happy life? Were you happy?"

"Quite, quite. I got used to a well-ordered life, it's only now the circumstances are hostile, only now I have to be a groom.

Isn't that right? I have quite a few years on me, my health is
bad, after a life like mine how else could my health be? My legs
still hold me up, though, thank you very much."

He took another cookie.

"Are you here for long?"

"Where else am I supposed to go? I can't go back, I burned
my ships. They're not expecting me. It was a rash step, of
course, but I was dependent on people there, too. The letter
seemed like it was from family, it even touched me a little. I
gave it to Admiral von Magen to read—a brilliant mind! I said
to him: Your Excellency, a sixth sense is drawing me to Paris.
I'm not going to get another chance. And he said to me: Your
Excellency, if it really is a sixth sense, then don't ignore it. That
was how we ruined Russia, by ignoring our sixth sense."

He became agitated suddenly, his neck turned red and
stretched.

"But they're telling me, Uncle, you misunderstood us.
They say, We didn't invite you to come, we just wanted to find
out about you."

"It's my fault," she said. "I was the one who lured you here."

He failed to understand and remained agitated.

"I very much wanted to see you one more time," she went
on. "I couldn't believe all that could be over forever. Ever since
April, when I learned you were alive and it was possible we
might see each other, it's hard to believe how much I've thought
about you. Don't be surprised that I'm talking this way. Now
there's been a revolution, now we stand naked before one another, there are no more secrets, nor could there be. That's why I'm
talking this way. I'm very much to blame for everything, I've
upset you greatly."

He coughed and looked to the side, still not fully compre-
hending her. With an effort she removed the tight sapphire ring
from her finger and caught his gaze again with her slow eyes.

"Here," she said quietly, "here is your ring. They might
give you a lot of money for it. I don't need it. My son will be a
Frenchman soon and an engineer. Only the others don't have to
know about this."

He blushed a furious red and began grinding his teeth so
hard that his long flat ears even started going up and down.

"Permit me, but no, how could I? Only a scoundrel would
take money from a woman."

"All three times they gave me a little over five thousand for
it at the pawn shop," she said in her deep half-whisper. "There's
been a revolution. We're all naked. Now we can do anything.
Take it."

She held the ring out to him.

"If you've become dependent on anyone, then it's my fault.
Forgive me, I'm repaying you with the ring. I wanted to see you
so much, I looked forward to it so much, that I disturbed your
peace."

He took the ring and squeezed it in his hand, and on that
hand, which had lost its former appearance, a vein popped up
like a fork. He wanted to speak but couldn't think of anything
to say, and he could not take his now piercing blue eyes off her.
She looked at her hand for a long time, at where the ring had
been. There, around her finger, was a light band of white that
would probably not last long. Then she turned her hand over and
began examining her broad palm with the lines she had known
for so long, until Murochka and Murochka came in, anxious but
happy, and Roman Germanovich with a spot on his knee.

"If you aren't afraid of a draft, uncle, we could open the window here," said Murochka.

Kryatov was thinking about something else and did not at first reply.

"Fine," he said all of a sudden, biting his lips. "Open your windows and your doors, have children. I'm moving."

"Where?" exclaimed the Murochkas.

He went into the vestibule and from there to the kitchen, where his things lay—a small dented basket, the satin box with his medals, a silver knob from a nonexistent cane—and started leaving the apartment.

Murochka came out after him into the vestibule and stood there and watched, trying to make sense of it.

"Listen, uncle," he said as if he were insulted. "I'm the one who's going to have to pay the bill at the Caprice. What ever have you dreamed up? What are you going to use for money?"

But Kryatov was already on the stairs with his creaking basket. Instead of a hat he had on a cap with a shiny visor. At the first step he stopped, turned around, his face taut, and madness flashed in his eyes.

"I'll go through my inheritance!" he cried, and a shudder ran through him. "They wanted to send me off to be a groom! I'll hire my own grooms to keep people like you from crossing my threshold!"

Murochka pulled her husband inside the door. And slammed it.

"This is going to cost us!"

"Stop it!" Murochka pressed herself against him and even held his ear lobe, like during their first days of marriage. "He has something stashed away, you could tell right off. People like that always have something stashed away."

All this was making Roman Germanovich uncomfortable. It was no accident that he had a Teutonic name; people with Teutonic names are often made to feel uncomfortable over other people.

"Goodbye, goodbye," he rustled. "Please, come see us, and be sure to bring your little one. We're very very grateful."

Née-Bychkova might not have even heard Kryatov threatening to hire grooms; not that her mind was not really on him anymore. She stepped into the vestibule, too. A circle had closed for her, a wide, noisy, difficult, and happy circle. The couple went outside, into the stifling city street on that hot summer's night. They didn't have far to go. She walked in step with him, her spouse. All these years she had been matching her step to his, like a frame to a doorpost. There were very few people about, on the whole way back they encountered only a couple of people, two women, no one else.

But the women were some of those who had arrived just the week before in gypsy wagons and were camped on the riverbank. Coins hung from the necks and wrists of these unwashed women, who were probably from Bessarabia itself, and their red skirts with dark blue flowers swirled around their knees as they walked. One of the women was old and very brown and wore round gold earrings, a green kerchief on her head, and goatskin shoes. The other was young and wore red high-heeled shoes, a straight part in her hair, and an embossed silver belt that cinched her waist. When she saw Roman Germanovich, who looked terribly Russian, even for Billancourt, if I can put it that way, the younger one stepped right in his path, placed her long narrow hand with the jangling bracelets on his sleeve, and looked him in the eyes in a gypsy way.

"Give me something, and I'll read your long life, grand-dad," she said in a singing voice. "Cross my palm and I'll tell you the whole truth, about whether your sweetheart is planning to cheat on you. Give me something."

She was slender, merry, and vociferous. On her shoulders she wore a bright, sunflower-yellow shawl whose soiled, curly fringe kept catching on the buckle of her burning hot belt.

1930

The Phantom of Billancourt

The day Nadia Basistova, tall skinny Nadezhda Ivanovna Basistova with the knot of fair hair at her nape, died, the Konoteshenkos, husband and wife, sent word to her husband, the father of her son, in Creusot. Despite the fact that her husband had thrown Nadia out because of her cheating, the Konoteshenkos knew it was time for Nikolai Basistov to come and devote himself to his son, who had been put for a few days into a shelter where they wouldn't keep the talkative, silly little boy for long.

The Konoteshenkos felt that Basistov was guilty all around for his wife's behavior, and when Nadia had arrived two years before and rented a room from them, explaining that she simply could not go back to her husband in Creusot, they had openheartedly replied that they considered her Basistov worse than a beast.

Nadia dreamed of becoming a maid, of wearing spanking clean clothes, ironing other people's silk undergarments, cleaning other people's shiny shoes, counting the silver and serving all kinds of rich dishes over the shoulders of anonymous guests.

But her son made that impossible, so she gave up thinking about what only the select few get to have in life and went to work at the factory, where she wore wide trousers cinched up above her waist and picked and sorted through the metal confetti that spilled into her hands from a wide pipe.

In the evenings men would call on her, and then she would gather up Lenka and the mattress he slept on, carry them out into the vestibule, and lay them out there on the floor. And if the Konoteshenkos happened to come into the vestibule during the night, they would curse Nikolai Basistov at length and with deep satisfaction for ruining Nadia's life. And they were filled with a soul-stirring joy at having concurred on this now and for all time.

Her guests were polite, did not ask for strong drinks, and took what they were served, mostly sweet wine. They came and went cautiously, holding the door so it wouldn't slam, and demonstrated a perfect understanding of the situation.

And then Nadia caught cold and died, and died so fast they didn't even have time to try to get her treated, time to ask her whether she wanted a doctor or an aspirin. What else were they to do with Lenka, who laughed so loud the whole building could hear? The Konoteshenkos buried her at the French bureaucracy's expense—she was a single factory worker, after all—and sent word to Creusot. They found Basistov's address in Nadia's things.

Men kept coming and asking for her for a few more days, incredulous and begging not to be made fun of. One, who brought a little something to eat, got quite angry and ordered them to tell Nadezhda he wasn't an idiot and he wouldn't let her treat him this way, he would get to her. But getting to her evidently was no longer possible. The Konoteshenkos cursed the visitors and told each other in an outburst of passionate unanimity that they had never known there were so many of *those men*.

Nikolai Basistov left for Paris the fifth day after the funeral, after making hasty arrangements. He felt both grief and anger toward his wife, who never had asked his forgiveness. From the very first day of his lonely life without her, he had been waiting for that hour, her arrival, or at least a letter. These two years had been filled to the brim with waiting. His entire life had been an unbroken and, as it now turned out, pointless wait. He didn't need anyone but her in the whole world, and because his thoughts ran constantly upon her, because in his poor imagination he kept composing future conversations with her, tiresome conversations, he had never actually been truly alone. He stubbornly told himself the same thing over and over: he wasn't the kind of man you could forget, they always came back to men like him, a sweet moment awaited him in life: forgiving her and letting her live with him.

When he arrived in Paris it was night. He had never been here before. He and two thousand others like himself had been sent straight from Turkey to the steel foundries. It had been his business to stay put and wait, he didn't even change rooms in Creusot for fear of being lost to Nadia, of her coming or writing and not finding him. So he stayed put, despite the fact that the people around him, who knew them both, were a drain on him, poisoning his life. He had to explain to each one of them that she hadn't left him, rather he had thrown her out.

He hadn't dared to show his face in Paris for fear of running into his wife and having her decide he had repented. He

thought: I'll come out of the station, stop at a shop, or go somewhere to eat, and there she'll be. The city may be big, but
there's no avoiding coincidences. Pride would be painted all
over her face (why should he afford her such pleasure?), and he
would have to come up and explain as she smiled: Don't think
I came after you.

And now he had seen Paris. He had seen the mailbox, the
wet street, the ugly face of a cart horse right above his ear, and
the long string of taxicabs under a long string of powerful
streetlamps. In the darkness, from above, from the heavenly
night, fragile snowflakes came sprinkling down to melt on his
lips and hands, so tender and fuzzy that a preoccupied person
could be forgiven for not noticing them at all. An elderly gentleman festooned with military honors opened his umbrella,
unable to decide whether it was raining or snowing. He could
see the sidewalk getting damp, but it never occurred to him to
look up. The old news seller, with her collapsed nose and eyes
red from crying, shielded her stack of evening papers from the
damp with the hem of her skirt.

Basistov walked past the line of taxicabs, looking for someone to ask the way, thinking he would find among the excel-
lently courteous, red-faced mustache wearers at least one
stranger with a familiar face. But there was no such face. The
dark roofs were getting a dusting of snow, and the stone buildings and broad sidewalks lent the capital grandeur. The fact that
Basistov's documents were in perfect order gave him courage for
a moment. He walked up to a policeman.

Basistov was short and a little bowlegged, and he wore a
straight part in his hair, which did little to flatter him. He was
carrying a medium-sized cardboard box tied with string and an

old umbrella with a lady's handle. He was persistent but not very clear, and the patrolman did not understand him right away.

It was quite far to Billancourt and the Place Nationale, and even Basistov had no idea how much time he spent underground on the train. He transferred twice, made one mistake, and had to climb out and ask the way. When Basistov finally came up for air everything was white with snow, it was nighttime, the stars were burning in the sky, and an ambulance with a little flag was racing into the wintry distance at full speed with a long, mournful clanging.

He walked down the poorly lit Russian streets. This was where she, his Nadia, must have darted in and out, pulling Lenka along, cursing her life. Where was the short pleated skirt she was wearing when he drove her out of the house, and where was the cute hat with the curved brim under which her fair curls tumbled onto her face? And the long fingers, so young and tender, with which, out of old habit, she sometimes covered her pale, frightened face? That is how Basistov had recalled her a hundred times and more all these years, and he knew, he knew for certain, that she would come to him because he was good, loyal, and loving, a little dishonest and pathetic, and cruel, but no more, after all, than all the others people go back to in the end. For two years he had had nothing but this confidence: of seeing Nadia's humiliation, hearing her voice when she said she had nowhere to go, she would be lost without him, if he didn't take her back she had only one end. Off three sides and into the pocket! His imagination was filled with this agonizing but happy picture, which, however, he had never really thought through completely.

A trolley with its conductors aboard went by, and a couple

whom it had not taken along on its journey watched yearningly, as it disappeared.

He rang at the apartment, they let him in, and he entered a room jammed with furniture, as if one thing after another had been stuffed in here willy-nilly: sideboard, chair, armchair, dresser. Konoteshenko's wife was sitting at the table, a not yet old, plump woman darning her husband's sky blue sock. Konoteshenko's place was opposite hers. There lay his newspaper—Russian, naturally—from which he chose to read aloud small announcements, funny bits like: "Looking for a son of Riurik on leave and ready for anything. Inquire in the second courtyard, back door . . ." or "I come to your house. I bring ultraviolet rays. Distances don't bother me. Guarantee . . ." Konoteshenko read them out loud, and his wife sat there and smiled.

Walking in, Basistov thought: "This, this is where she lived, died, and walked, this is where they carried her out," and both Konoteshenkos stood on either side of him and looked at him sadly. He was exactly as Nadia had described him.

"A lonely young woman in our hard times," said the Konoteshenko wife with dramatic pauses, and she lowered her eyes so as not to see Basistov's face, "cast on the tyranny of fate with a child. . . ."

Basistov's face darkened.

". . . when you have no money, no one to protect you, and you don't know where to go or how to feed yourself, and you have no warm coat, and all in all . . ."

"Where's Lenka?" asked Basistov.

"Lenka's in a shelter. But they won't keep him there long," said Konoteshenko himself. "It's for temporary residents."

"They took him because we asked the priest. He's a good man, he set it all up. He says there's no rush to pick him up, he can stay a week or so."

"But it's been eight days already."

"Ten."

"Nine."

"Well, all right. They'll keep him a little longer, if you want you can pick him up, if you want you can wait a couple of days."

"Why wait? I'm a working man, I have to get back to Creusot. They dock me for every day. It's a short conversation. I can't be sitting around."

" . . . in these times," said the wife, "to be thrown out on the street. It could only end in death. But, of course, some people will never understand, they'll live their lives and never figure it out, never repent."

Basistov said sullenly: "Please don't preach to me. I did not throw her and the child out, I only threw her out. If she had left me Lenka, things would have been easier for her. What, do you think I should have forgiven her? On the basis of what morality?"

"You only threw her out?" the two voices said together. "Do you think she could have lived without Lenka? If you had seen how she carried him out into the vestibule on his mattress at night, you would have realized that she couldn't live without him."

"You're only saying that because she's dead, but if she'd married here you wouldn't have considered me a beast."

"Married!" the wife exclaimed. "How could she have married? She didn't have that kind of soul. She was a bird. Her soul was a bird of paradise. That kind isn't made for marriage. And you ought to have understood that. If only you'd told her, That's the way nature made you, I'm not your judge, I love you, and we have a son, and I'll never leave you."

Basistov chuckled.

"There's morality for you. A lady's argument. It works out well for you, but we men come up short."

He gave Konoteshenko a challenging look, as if soliciting his support.

"Women can be different," Konoteshenko said diplomatically. "I think that if you can't understand a woman, it's better not to marry."

They took Basistov into Nadia's cold and empty room. Besides the couch and rack there were a hanging shelf that was now on the floor, a chair, and three empty Madeira bottles under the window in the corner. There was also Nadia's high trunk, which she had dragged with such difficulty to the station as the neighbors looked on merrily. She had pulled it with one hand and Lenka with the other. Such was the picture. It had been broad daylight, and it was better to forget it altogether. After the Konoteshenkos left, he pushed the trunk into the middle of the room, sat down beside it on a chair, and opened it.

It smelled of Nadia's sickly sweet perfume which she had been given God only knew when—by whom? The lover he had seen her with probably. This perfume permeated her, her things, her life, and ultimately it choked her. In this fragrance now lay all kinds of women's clothing that had once been useful and now was hard to understand. Here was a black silk dress, mended and shiny from wear, and holey stockings, and a scrap of something in a rotted, faded hat. There were Lenka's old hobnailed shoes, and a lace handkerchief, and a purse made of oilskin stamped with a crocodile pattern, and a broken comb.

The more he dug in the trunk, the more strongly he felt he was not just digging but trying to find something incriminating, disgraceful, shameful, some letter, or money, or something gold, so that he could say: See, she took gifts, too, she must have lived merrily. But she had left behind no gold, no money, no stack of papers. Whether she had loved anyone, or how she loved, or why she lived the way she did remained unknown. Only the three Madeira bottles brazenly testified to the fact that someone very recently had drunk in this room, sipping quietly in solitude, or pouring it down the hatch with a friend.

He walked into the Konoteshenkos' room without knocking. The husband was lying in bed under a blanket intently watching his wife undress. Her arms were bare and her round white elbows were stretched behind her as she tried to unfasten the button at the back of her brassiere.

"So why, if things were so bad for her, why didn't she come back and beg for forgiveness?" Basistov asked crudely. "I might have forgiven her, maybe I suffered, too."

Konoteshenko's wife was dumbfounded.

"She never thought about that. Go out into the vestibule. Please don't come in without knocking. That never even occurred to her."

Konoteshenko turned over under the blanket.

"An incredible question! She never even mentioned Creusot."

Basistov was still standing in the vestibule when the Konoteshenkos slammed the door shut behind him and locked it with a key. He went back to Nadia's room and sat down on the couch, and a strange feeling came over him. Suddenly it seemed as if it were he who had come to see her instead of her coming to see him, that he wanted her to listen to him, to speak to her of

his love, ask her forgiveness, beg her to come back to him. In this
odd torpor, neither pride nor vanity existed at all, nor a sense of
insult, only despair that she was gone and he couldn't tell her
that he didn't care how she'd been living these two years or with
whom, whom she drank the Madeira with or embraced on the
couch. He had come to ask her not to push him away, and it did-
n't matter where she went after she examined herself in the mirror, narrow-hipped, long-legged, close-mouthed as always. He
wouldn't ask any questions, and when she came back he would-
n't say anything either, he would just be happy to see her.

This torpor passed as suddenly as it had come, though. He
came around and thought he might have fallen asleep sitting up
on the couch. In front of him was the trunk with the rummaged-
through things, and the window, beyond which hung the night
and the murky moon and snow melting on the roofs. He was
alone, and there wasn't going to be any meeting here or there.
There wasn't anyone there at all, as he had long suspected and
now saw clearly.

In the morning, before going to work, the Konoteshenkos
warned him that they were trusting him, a stranger, entirely
with the apartment and key, but in Billancourt the police knew
each and every person, in general. They left. And Basistov went
straight into their room to find out what kind of people they
were. He looked at everything and found lots of locked doors and
drawers, but there were interesting photographs on the wall,
faded and dusty, which he began examining. In some stood men
with and without beards, arms hanging at their sides, hair cut in
a fringe, wearing tall boots and embroidered shirts, and the
broad-cheeked women sat wearing wide jackets, their hair
combed very simply. In others the men wore frock coats (one had

pince-nez) and the women wore their hair styled in the old-fashioned way, and dresses with narrow waists. Basistov couldn't
decide which of the two Konoteshenkos had married down. On
the sideboard lay yesterday's bread, and Basistov couldn't resist,
he ate it all. He didn't find anything else in the sideboard. He
went into the kitchen and drank the rest of the milk. He looked
out the window. Not a trace, not a strip, was left of yesterday's
snow. Everything was black, wet, and dull.

He went out to roam the streets and squares where old
maids from the Salvation Army were handing out flyers to
passers-by, where Kozlobabin was opening his store and unload-
ing goods, where he could hear a hoarse gramophone blaring
somewhere. He walked past the brick walls behind which the
factory stood, but it was deserted and silent at that hour. He
went to pick up Lenka and thought about how he wouldn't recognize him, wouldn't be able to pick him out of the crowd of
children, and if they gave him someone else's child instead of
Lenka that wouldn't be so bad but it would certainly make for
all kinds of red tape and folderol.

He opened the gate, walked through a square courtyard
hemmed in by five-story buildings, and walked up the porch
steps. The parquet gleamed and he smelled barley soup. Upstairs,
the children's voices were quiet and polite as they recited either
a poem or a prayer. He was led into the dining room, where azure
drawings hung on the walls—rugs, people, and sailboats. Out
the window he saw a mailman and a cat ran by. The director came
in and the children tumbled in after her from upstairs. They
brought Lenka to him; his nose was running but he was alive and
well, and neither had any difficulty recognizing the other. "This
is your papa," the director said, nonetheless. "Say, 'Hello, papa.'"

Lenka's face now seemed to Basistov more like his than before. In any case, it was his son, he scarcely doubted it. He kissed him on the head, and Lenka laughed his quick wild laugh and asked why had he come and would he be going away soon. Life turned out not to be as simple as Basistov had thought. Life could get unusually complicated all of a sudden. He stuffed Lenka's belongings into his pockets and took his son outside.

First they went for a walk, sat on the boulevard, and ate breakfast. Then they went to the Konoteshenkos' and napped, and as soon as they were rested they started talking. Basistov was looking Lenka over, and Lenka was looking Basistov over. The conversation turned to Nadia, of course, and Basistov said that tomorrow morning they would go to Creusot together, where Nadia was waiting for him. Lenka was a little frightened that she would go even farther away without waiting for them and shouldn't they set out today, but Basistov reassured him. Then, stuffing a chocolate into Lenka's mouth, he sat Lenka on his knee, plucked up his courage, and started grilling him: How did he and his mama live, what did they eat, where did they go, did they argue? And Lenka answered everything the same way: They lived wonderfully, they ate a lot, they went to church, and they never argued. And then he burst into tears and started kicking Basistov, and when Basistov asked whether he remembered him he sobbed angrily, screaming, "No, no, no!"

Nadia had taught Lenka this, of course. It was perfectly obvious to Basistov that she hadn't needed him and he must have only gotten in the way of her scandalous behavior. She must have lived cheerfully, drunkenly, she must have been kept by some Billancourt businessman or robbed someone in a drunken scam. In short, she obviously hadn't needed his forgiveness, and Basistov found it unbelievable that on the night of his arrival he could have had those incredibly tearful words for her, that he could humiliate himself and despair, or regret, anything. He drove out the thought of last night, when he had sat in front of the open trunk. Thank God she was dead. Otherwise what would he have done with her? If she had had the soul of a bird of paradise, imagine the trouble, the agony he would have had with that bird! Without her death, many long years might have passed in Creusot and he would have still been sitting there waiting, like a fool.

It was twilight now and snowing again, but this time mixed with rain. Lenka was playing with his old boots, putting them on his hands, getting down on all fours and saying, "Papa, I'm a lion." Basistov listened for the others, paced around the room, went into the vestibule, and warmed himself by the cast-iron stove. Lenka crawled after him on all fours: "Papa, I'm a tiger." When the Konoteshenkos came home, hungry, tired, and amorous, he couldn't warm himself any more. He decided to leave that day and not wait until morning. Take the night train.

Before leaving the apartment, he went to say goodbye. "We'll have supper at the station, board, and be off," he said. Lenka was on the verge of crying but managed not to. The Konoteshenkos were cool with Basistov but tender with Lenka. There was nothing more to say. He apologized for eating their bread, he hadn't thought they might need it, in his absent-mindedness, forgive me. . . . They tickled Lenka behind the ears. At the last minute he remembered that he'd also drunk their milk, but didn't say anything. He and Lenka both went down the stairs, and the door slammed shut behind them.

1931

Kolka and Liusenka

W/e're still alive!

By this I don't mean that none of us lost his life this past year. No, the knife, the sleeping powders, the gas, they all did their job. The bullet inserted itself into the heart (in dark moments a military man will be drawn to the bullet even in old age). There were natural deaths, too, in apartment houses, on the street, in the hospital. First the colonels and lieutenant colonels started going, and now the captains are getting to be that age (I'm not counting the generals, who took a seat behind the wheel and are still there). There have also been instances you can't explain: a man was buried who had known what to do, who had already been saved and resuscitated and rolled away, and then one day a room or apartment was transformed for a few hours into a sinking ship, a derailed train, a burning house. It's happened. . . . No matter, though, we're still alive!

The sounds of a gramophone cut through the murky rain, the nasty daytime weather, from the Cabaret—Chopin's funeral march or the "Muzhik from Kamarinsk" rearranged as a foxtrot. In the twilight, as evening falls, Madame Klava's girl in her kerchief runs out again over the slippery sidewalk to fetch bread from the bakery, where yellow balls glitter on an artificial velvet tree that hasn't been taken down since Christmas. The wind flies off the river, decrepit plane trees whip their branches against the sky, and his new hometown breaks someone's heart. Sure, there are people in Paris and other cities who are equally aware of their irreparable lives, but there's not room for all that's irreparable in our own Billancourt.

Many of us have breathed, sighed, and gasped here. In the autumn, leaves rustle on the square; in the summer dust swirls against the pediments of the Renault factory and the children cough; in the spring the men who are out of work go to the riverbank and there they lie for a long time, eyes closed. As the sun makes its heavenly circuit overhead, they slip newspapers under their heads and stretch out their identical bare yellow feet. Every day, as evening falls, when the three distant smokestacks that hold up our whole Billancourt sky turn purple, dissolve, disappear, and then settle more solidly in the sunset, every day a woman walks past these identical feet, past the linen hung out to dry, goes around to the men lying there with her shaving basin, brush, and razor and shaves them for five sous (they sit up a little then, and she soaps them over and over, lathers them with her brush; she herself is dark, skinny, and old). Every day little girls excited by the spring and the city go strolling; squealing young ladies run hither and yon. And young matrons—who were once those same little girls and young ladies, of course—gaze tranquilly and gravely into the distance as they push their children in strollers. And quite a few have yellow Chinese babies in their strollers and two or three toddlers walking alongside, hanging on to their mother's skirt.

Sometimes a Negro baby peeks out of a stroller, pale from his mother's milk, and sometimes simply one of ours, a white French baby.

That was spring, and all summer there was more blue sky, more sun, and the smell of machine oil wafting through the streets, the beating of the factory's heart behind the high walls, the heat, the monotony of the harsh workdays and the pointless, impoverished, and savage merriment of Sundays. At first they worked five and a half days, then five, then four, then three and a half days a week. August! In Europe, there is no sadder month in the year!

Maybe this warmth, these clouds in the sky, all those seas and cottages, the distant roads, suit someone. They do soothe the souls of civilians and ladies, but military men don't care for them. And when suddenly with the crash of steel and a two-finger whistle the first October wind comes swooping down with its darkness and rain and its extended melancholy, our hearts start spinning in place again, their own place in the chest.

Attention! (We clear our throats.) Don't let anyone see! (We stand straighter.) Close ranks! If you were ever made of water and salt, then that's long past. Now you have to be made of pig iron.

And so—we're alive. And it's January already. Autumn whizzed by, but Christmas dragged on, raining the whole time. And so it is sometimes, due to the raw softness in the air, on an evening with stars, or without, that the first hint of spring begins to creep into the soul. People tell us to seek an explanation for this fact in a certain world crisis.

But actually . . . Those who have settled neatly on the benches of the square and who have never had either a parlor or a dining room, they probably do often dream of spring, when you can eat less and drink more (water, after a pickle). This way of living does suit some people. Right now they lie around all day gnawed by the cold, and at night they go somewhere—to a building under construction, or an empty trolley booth, behind a fence—and people like that naturally require resort temperatures. They just do! Bring on the spring! Whereas we who have heat at home and souls still prepared to take on God knows what, we try not to soften, sour, or coddle ourselves with vegetables, lilac, and nightingales.

What about Veslovsky? What does he want? Is this man really never going to speak up! He has a stove, and he heats that stove at least every other day. He has a bed, albeit a narrow one, but a fine bed, and he sleeps in it—we know that, too, because at night we can hear its creak and his long, dry cough. They say it's not so terrible because Veslovsky is no longer young. He's old: he's fifty-three.

It should be said at the outset that this is an unusual individual. In the past, there were rumors going around about what a scoundrel he had been. There was some story about him and two girls at Mineralnye Vody and about him shooting some official at the last moment in Batumi; in Constantinople he was caught in the diamond merchants' affair, but the diamonds' trail went cold. Much later, in Paris, in about 1928, one small stone sparkled in the knot of his tie, but it was soon lost. He worked for a certain Franco-Russian institution where he was kept on for his manners, his French, and the deftness with which he pushed out all the former Russian employees—until they pushed him out as well. Everyone was sick and tired of him. The typist took him to court over certain improprieties, and something had been erased in the accounts book. He descended the staircase as if he was an actor in a theater, a beaten man now, his coat instantly worn and rusty. When he slammed the door a piece of plaster fell on his shoulder, just like in an novel.

And suddenly it was clear—on the streets, at home, in certain offices he called at—he was an old man, a very old man. No trace remained of his former manner and agility, all he had left was his French, which seemed ridiculous in someone so tattered and so long unshaven. Most important, from the back his head looked like a balding monkey's. Here and there hair lay in clumps on his collar, sprinkling dandruff; here and there you could see a bald spot, even several bald spots, thinning his once mighty head of hair. He had always been slender, he had even been handsome, they said, and had worn a monocle. He had carried fine perfumed handkerchiefs as large as napkins. Once upon a time.

What's so unusual about this? Indeed, so far it's all perfectly ordinary: a man once insolent, a so-called gentleman of noble blood and loutish behavior, goes downhill and gets lost in life— that's nothing! But the thing is that Veslovsky did have something in his current life that was worth telling.

To begin with, on Sundays a girl and a boy came to visit him, and not only did these children always visit him separately, most importantly neither the girl nor the boy had the least inkling of the other's existence. The girl came in the morning at about eleven, stayed less than an hour, and went home for lunch. The boy came after two and left at about five. Both called Veslovsky "Papa" or even "Papochka;" they were his children by different mothers.

The girl was fifteen or so, but in her winter coat, on a gentle day when there was still a trace of white snow on the roofs and people were on their way to church, she seemed like a fine young lady. When she rang the bell, he hurried through his empty apartment to the door (his landlords were already at mass), let her in, and kissed her cautiously on the cheek.

"Hello, Liusenka."

And each time he felt as if he would be happy forever because she had come, even though she came in vain.

She was a rich girl, and he was embarrassed to have her see him in his impoverished state. She wore bright, cheerful dresses and bobbed her hair. She sat down on his bed and unwrapped her purchases, and it was always something surprising she had bought in a good grocery store, somewhere very far away, in another world where none of us has ever strayed. We may only have seen shop windows like that in passing, windows where sausages hang, sausage windows that made our hearts race. Others' hearts race at flower windows, or shoe windows, there are probably even eccentrics whose heartd flutter at the sight of a bookstore. But on a raw, pitch-black street, on a night in the capital when everything is in its place—the lilac shadows, the orange lights—when a happy hour arrives for someone, we look at the ham, at the crocks of pâté, at the dressed fish, and we can't tear ourselves away.

Then she took out twenty-five francs and gave them to Veslovsky. He knew it was her own money, and he hesitated before accepting the bills and tucking them in his wallet. He put the coffeepot on the burner and washed two cups, and he smoked. She told him everything he was allowed to know, culling from the past week what was most uninteresting, most general; he did not need to know anything else. Her mother and stepfather she touched on only lightly in a story, in passing. They were going to the mountains to the snow and she was staying behind with her fox terrier and the English maid (who, by the way, was sitting in a café right now waiting for her).

"Have you any beaux yet?" he asked with a grimace, and she said: "A whole slew of them."

She grew bored very quickly, and, not knowing what else she could tell him about and remembering all the while that there were many, many things she had promised never ever to speak of, she began despite everything to tell him about her mother, her house, her stepfather, her school. Her mother! He reminded himself that she was talking about Lida, the very woman for whose sake twenty years ago he had attempted suicide and who had ultimately left him, obtained a divorce, and vanished from his life.

"Well, Papa, I'll be going," she said, glancing at the watch on her narrow wrist. "Papa, you should . . ."

But she stopped herself.

"Thank you Liusenka," he said. "Ask there, if you can, whether Vsevolod Petrovich has an old suit. Be sure to ask, don't forget, and I'll come by, they can leave it with the doorman."

This was her father, the one who had given her carriage rides in Petersburg, in the carriage her mama's feathered hat wouldn't fit into once because the door was too narrow for it. How many discussions of this there had been subsequently! She knew she came here not casually but under an agreement, decided by the court, that was how her mother had once explained it to her. This was how it had to be. He held her gloves while she tightened the narrow buckle of her belt. And then she left, tall beyond her years, her entire appearance like a particularly graceful amphora, or perhaps a flowering vine, or he knew not what.

He had his lunch and washed the dishes, then hastily read the newspaper. In the next room his landlords were having their lunch, or their dinner perhaps. They always took a long time and ate in silence. Even though on Sundays the whole family got together, eight of them at least, you couldn't hear their voices because everyone was concentrating on the food, and this occupation went on for at least two hours interrupted only by the sound of dishes clattering in the kitchen.

The doorbell woke Veslovsky and his landlords opened the door. Kolka walked down the dark hallway to Veslovsky's door, scratched around a while, unable to find the handle right away in the darkness, entered without knocking, and threw himself on his father's neck, clambered onto his lap, grabbed his pale, flat ears, and all this with such laughter, such a ray of light in his eyes, that Veslovsky began laughing awkwardly, too, hugging his son, who smelled of the street and laundry soap.

One of Liusenka's tens went immediately into Kolka's fist, then he polished off the chicken and the strip of bacon.

"You must really be a millionaire!" he exclaimed. "I told them at home you're a millionaire, you eat tasty things, but they say you're going to be begging on the *parvis* pretty soon. What's a *parvis*? There's no such French word. Is that Russian? Give me a cig? That's okay, I just said that to scare you. Yesterday I snitched an apple from Kozlobabin's store."

He threw himself across the bed and guffawed and pulled up his feet, still in their wood-soled shoes. Veslovsky could almost count the shiny nails.

"It's a sin to steal," he said. "They put you in prison for that."

"Uncle says you've been stealing your whole life but you didn't go to prison."

"Don't you speak up for me, Kolenka?"

"But what if it's true? Hell if I know!"

He slid off the bed, sat in Veslovsky's lap, and put his open palm on Veslovsky's bald head.

"You smell like perfume," he said suspiciously. "A millionaire bathes in perfume."

This one came not because of the court, this one came because he wanted to. There had been no marriage, no divorce. It had all been very brief, hasty, really. Nonetheless, this was his son. That he knew.

One hand held on tight to the ten he'd been given, the other touched absolutely everything: the greasy velvet pillow, the shaving brush, the old travel guide. What amazed him most was the size of the room. He himself lived not far away, in one single room separated from the kitchen by a curtain, and in it lived his mother, the man he called uncle, he himself, and his two stepsisters, ages three and two.

Veslovsky sat and thought how much Kolka looked like his mother. The same ardent eyes and turned-up nose, the same fair hair. Enough! Had all this happened? Even dreams left more of themselves behind than did his memories from the his past. If it weren't for Kolka, he might have thought there was nothing to remember at all—and really, when you came right down to it, what was left by now? Everything had melted away, the years had passed, and nothing remained. Pardon me, why nothing? Weren't the gray hair, the wrinkles, the cough at night, the sciatica plenty? He was missing seven teeth and when he read he needed glasses. Wasn't that enough?

In damp weather his knees throbbed. Coffee made his heart pound.

It was hard to get Kolka to leave. A promise of the zoo, a promise of a carriage ride in the Bois de Boulogne, a promise of a soccer match. Suddenly, a bizarre idea occurred to Veslovsky. Before he could think it over he snatched at it.

"Next Sunday come in the morning. I want to introduce you to a certain girl. Want to?"

(He was going to regret this. He was sure he was doing something stupid.)

"Why not in the afternoon? Are you going away?"

"No, just because."

"I'll tell them you're going away. That you're flying overseas in an airplane. Won't they be surprised!"

"But why do that?"

"I'll tell them you went to buy an automobile."

"Fine then, tell them that."

When they were saying goodbye Veslovsky gave Kolka a sip of wine. Kolka swallowed noisily, rubbed his tummy, and grinned from ear to ear. Then Veslovsky was alone.

He realized full well that nothing good would come of this meeting, that he was proceeding to destroy his life and was even taking pleasure in doing so. The visits might stop. He had initiated a dangerous game, and this time he wouldn't get out of the water dry. It served him right! It all depends on who and what shapes a man: he doesn't always want what's best for himself, he just might want—and even actively seek—harm. What does he care about the harm, the evil, the losses and failures, the confusions and disgraces? Everything had been destroyed, and he felt like smashing the last shard, crushing it, pulverizing it.

There was still time to fix things, yes, he could easily fix things, but he didn't want to fix anything. He had grabbed this glimmer of an idea by the tail and was now hanging by it over an abyss. But did it really matter? Loud words had ceased to mean anything. There was no such abyss. It was all trivial, inconsequential. Not even worth thinking about.

On Saturday evening he visited a certain club where he rarely went and where they were not happy to see him. There had even been talk about how it was time to expel him and take away his membership card. Let him go to the four winds. At the club he listened to the conversations—the same old conversations and discussions of the Romanov tricentennial. He retained his own private opinion and everyone ignored him. He coughed a lot that night, switched on the light, and paced. In the morning he cleaned up, removed a spiderweb from the corner at the ceiling. He lit the stove. And when warmth started coming from it he felt like going back to sleep and not responding to anyone's knock.

"Today, Liusenka," Veslovsky said quietly, "a little boy is coming to visit. His manners aren't very good because he's poor. You see, Liusenka, I was married after you all threw me out. This boy is my son, so to speak, by my second marriage."

"Ah," said Liusenka, and she unwrapped a large package in brown paper. From it she took out a kilo of tea sausage, a jar of preserves, and gray striped trousers.

"You don't mind?"

"No, why should I? Everyone has children. Why didn't you tell me this a long time ago?"

"I was afraid you'd find it strange."

"No, I don't care. Are you going to make coffee?"

"There isn't any coffee. There's tea."

"Try on the trousers."

It really did seem as if she didn't care, but suddenly she was terribly bored in this dusty, cold room, and she felt like going home. After all, she had come here not only because the court had so decided, she thought she was condescending, that she was the only one, so smart and good, who cared about his life of poverty. She was probably his sole joy, and that was nice to know. And now? It turned out she wasn't the only one, there was someone else. She felt like smashing something, saying something spiteful, but she refrained so she wouldn't burst into tears.

"No, they're small on you," she said cruelly, looking at Veslovsky, for whom Lida's husband's trousers were just the ticket.

"No, not at all! They're a perfect fit."

"No, I can see they're small on you. I'll take them back."

"Liusenka, not a stitch! I don't even have to let them down."

"No, no, you can't see from the back. They'll rip by evening. Take them off."

He went into the corner and changed. He didn't dare argue. The kettle boiled.

Kolka rang the doorbell and Veslovsky hurried out of the room.

"Sit down, Kolka. This is Liusenka. Say hello. I'll explain who she is later. Right now we're going to eat some sausage. Here's the tea, and here's the butter. Take off your coat, the stove is hot."

And the past Veslovsky was revisiting seemed amazingly

cozy. He could have sat like this to the end of his days: the girl, all smooth and educated and fed by someone else, with a governess and piano lessons; and the boy, a hungry but cheerful ragamuffin independent beyond his years who also, in general, was scarcely his concern.

But Kolka demanded mustard, and Liusenka drank her tea with a spoon, barely touching it with her lips.

He talked the whole time, told them everything he had heard, the Billancourt news that Kolka knew before he did and that was of no interest to Liusenka. She left quickly, wrapping up Vsevolod Petrovich's trousers in the same paper with her little white hands. She was unyeilding, even though Veslovsky said, darting around her, that he was just going to go to his landlords and bring back a measuring tape and show her, show her . . . But she knew for some reason that he wouldn't go to his landlords. She smiled, shook her head, and put the package under her arm. "That's what I thought," she said when she was in the vestibule. "He's fatter and taller than you, after all."

Kolka chuckled, took a piece of sausage off the table and sniffed it.

"She's the one who brings you this," flicking his thievish eyes toward the door, "and does she give you the tens, too?"

It was obvious he felt uncomfortable here today and he thought that home was better, the fumes of the perpetual laundering, his little sisters' wailing, his mother's shouting.

"A millionaire," said Kolka, and he went to put on his little coat. "Why do they say only others get their money from charity?" (He heard this exact phrase every day at home.) And seeing that Veslovsky had turned toward the window, his shoulders hunched and his head dropped, Kolka stuck the piece of sausage into his torn pocket and went out, his hobnails clicking, and slammed the door.

Now no one visits Veslovsky on Sundays. Instead, Kolka plays ball outside with his buddies, and the neighbors have already complained about them twice. Liusenka realizes he's not going to go to court; he doesn't have any money for a lawyer. She goes for a drive instead. Kolka doesn't recognize his father when he walks by, and Veslovsky now spends the entire day on his feet because he delivers the milk to the apartment houses.

He did get a pair of trousers, though, nearly new, through the efforts of our committees.

1933

The Violin of Billancourt

I t's still the same.

Yet it has had to change a little. Had to because it has no monuments, no fountains, no bell towers, none of those ornaments on which any ordinary city built for eternity rests. Instead it has a grocer's, a Polish tavern (in what was once a church), a nightclub, a hairdresser's, and factory gates where a barrier with a red light is lowered during working hours, just like crossing on some long journey. Not by this does a city endure.

True, there are also four smokestacks holding up our Billancourt sky, as someone once said. In our city they take the place of columns, if I can put it that way. But can they really save the day and protect the city from weather and time? No, they cannot save the day.

The weather is cloudy and dark; it's always autumn here, unless it's hot. Time passes and everything changes. For Kozlobabin's grocery business, for Boris Gavrilovich's hairdressing salon, for the residents of the Hotel Caprice, for the clients of the nightclub (where the owner, by the way, has filled out markedly), three years passing here is like three thousand years for some caryatid or equestrian statue. Three years passing. . . . Once there was an accordion on the cross street and Shurochka stamped her heels there, a happy drunken voice bellowed "The Steward of Mariupol" across the Place Nationale, and at noon a crowd emerged like herring from the open-hearth furnaces and squealing transmissions, from that whole helllish factory, following their noses: for a little something to eat, a bite, a snack. This was life. Billancourt did not believe in tears. For a proper existence, for a place of their own in the world, people repaid the world with their labor, which smelled of sweat, garlic, and alcohol. This was life. But since then something in it had hesitated, as if a shudder had gone through the world's equilibrium. There can be no doubt of this, especially if you bear in mind that Misha Sergeich was walking down the street with a not altogether firm step, walking and carrying a violin.

Something had hesitated. And anyone who had been counting on people was a little worse off, and anyone who had been counting on God's mercy was all right, as always. But then there were the others whose hopes were on themselves, on their four limbs and their minds, and they may have been a little better off. In any case, Misha Sergeich was walking down the street with his violin.

Those who had counted on people now didn't care when people fired from their jobs rushed off to Paris or lay low at home, suddenly ceasing to have any need of de Gurevich the venerologist, or Sauset the dentist, or Gnutikov the solicitor, who had long since chosen chicken soup over eternity and now wore his felt shoes in all weather to cross the street for some tobacco. One fine rainy day, Boris Gavrilovich's hairdressing salon closed down, and dry goods were hanging over the door soon after: warm stockings, jerseys, and aprons. In place of Abdulaev's restaurant, where flaccid hunks of meat sprinkled with parsley always lay in the window, a shoe repair shop opened, and now shoes were set out there, soles up. Where there used to be a nightclub was now a laundry, and instead of the vacant lot not far from the Moonlight, where the owner had also put on some weight, instead of this vacant lot where they had once found a dead body, now stood a house built as an investment, which was empty and drafty. Not making a profit.

Yes, things had had to change a little. Why should they be any better for you or me? Our newspaper explains this by referring to the world crisis. Where it came from, where it first flourished, no one knows. Maybe in America. That's just a guess, though. Some things don't change: for instance, our unbreakable Billancourt moon and the carnival blockhead that people hit to test their strength. Could our accidentally beloved backwater really become different? In essence, it's still the same. Let them think, as they say, that because of this and that the end is coming to Billancourt. There is no end or limit to Billancourt, nor will there ever be.

Misha Sergeich was short and for this and no other reason Sonia had hesitated for many years. "Lord," she always thought, "why is he that height? Maybe I'll still meet someone I like just as much but someone taller. After all, he comes up quite literally to my shoulder." She lived in Paris and had a million illusions, whereas he lived in Billancourt and had a million agonies. They hadn't seen each other for eight months when she came to visit him.

He came home with his violin and they told him down-stairs that a lady was sitting in his room. Ladies did not visit him, and he worried: this wasn't his wife coming to see him, was it, the wife he hadn't seen for twelve years? They had part-ed in Africa. It turned out to be Sonia. Skinny, pale, and wear-ing something fancy and torn, she was sitting on his sofa.

"There's a story for you!" said Misha Sergeich, so overjoyed he had no idea what he was saying.

"The story lies ahead," said Sonia, very agitated. "I'll tell you a story right now."

He sat down on the chair and put two glasses and a bottle of ice-cold, tart red wine on the table. "Hello, hello," he said, "I'm listening."

"This is Paris speaking," she replied, wiping a tear from her eyelash and trying to keep her voice from shaking. "I haven't had a job since summer."

It was a short little story, and funny, but with a sad end-ing. Sonia had gone from being a salesclerk in the spring to working as a maid, a high-class maid, naturally, dressing a young lady (the lady turned out to have been Russian once), serving at the table, keeping the silver clean, and from time to time washing her silk stockings. Then the gentleman lost his money and everyone in the house was fired. They paid her off with a little rug and the tulle from the window in the dining room. She had been left like that in September. And now it was December.

Misha Sergeich offered her some wine but she refused. Then he drank some himself. He was silent for a while and then asked whether she knew how to sing. She said that depended and he got ready to listen some more.

But she didn't feel like going on with her story. It was about these three months that she was reluctant to speak. She asked: "Don't you come home for lunch anymore? And why is it four o'clock now and you're not at the factory?"

"I've changed profession," he said, "and the lunch hour is my busiest time."

She gave him a long, hard look, then shifted her eyes to the violin, which was stained too bright a color.

"You go around to courtyards?" she asked.

"Yes, I go around to courtyards."

At that she pulled out a handkerchief and started crying.

She cried for a long time, and he didn't try to console her, he didn't say anything cheerful, didn't try to play her a saucy foxtrot or a march like "Longing for Home." He didn't even offer her a drink. He sat in silence and looked at her long legs, the hands covering her face, her parcel, which in the gathering dusk seemed larger than it in fact was. When she was finished crying he stood up and walked to the window. An empty square, a fence, a bakery on the corner. He had seen all this before.

"Your arms are so skinny now," he said all of a sudden, "and so are your legs."

If a third party had heard this he probably would have thought these words beside the point. Especially about her legs. But they were alone, so he also said:"This is all temporary. It will be different. We'll think of something. Right now I'm going out to buy something. We'll have tea."

Outside it was true night as it can only be on a December afternoon, long before nightfall. There, on the left, the river had frozen to the embankment, which no one used this time of year, and here, on the square, by the lighted sausage shop, stood a derelict looking at the sausage. For the New Year, the confectioner's elaborately decorated window shone with a tinfoil star and gold and silver ribbon, and under the streetlamp stood a sooty child selling sclerotic roses to passersby, flowers that had been nipped by the frost that morning and were now halfway from the hothouse to the garbage heap. They were being bought up because of the holiday, the foil star, and the cheap sparkle.

It was dark in the room, and Misha Sergeich thought Sonia was gone. In the light, though, it turned out she was sitting right where she had been. And he realized that he had gone out to give her a chance to leave without any explanations if something was wrong. But she hadn't gone, and her parcel was in its place. He started fussing with the kettle and the burner, handsomely arranging cheese, ham, and bread on a piece of paper. Sonia ate. He sat across from her. He was so happy he felt like explaining a certain theory of his to her, but he didn't know how to begin.

"Have you been doing this for long?" she asked.

"Half a year."

"What do you play?"

"The classical repertoire. And military marches. Occasionally something light. There's a gypsy here, he has a guitar, he sings ballads. We try not to horn in on one another."

"You always knew how to play the violin."

"Oh, yes!" He wanted to tell her about how in Petersburg, when he was a student at the Psycho-Neurological Institute, he had had his own orchestra, but he decided he would tell her some other time.

He looked at her for a long while, not knowing whether to take her hand or not.

"I have this theory," he said finally, and he placed his hand on hers. "Lord, how skinny your fingers are!" Sonia shivered but didn't move. "This theory: We're not coming back to this earth. . . . Oh, my God, don't cry, I'm telling you something cheerful! We aren't coming back to this earth and we don't know any other and it's unlikely we ever will. You have to work from this assumption."

Two tears dropped from Sonia's eyes onto the ham.

"Give close thought to what I'm saying. This is very important."

She nodded.

"And once you get some rest . . . actually, later about that."

She looked at him silently, pensively. He moved closer to her.

"I can change my repertoire."

She didn't say anything.

"I can switch to ballads. If you agree to sing. It's not at all frightening. And you know, I'm certain this is only temporary."

She nodded and smiled.

"Just now, when I was coming back from the square, I saw a couple pushing a cart, a husband and wife, a cart piled with all kinds of junk, which they set up for business by the factory in the evening. You know, they looked so happy pushing it together, their hands held on as solidly and as tightly as they did to each other."

"They won't let us."

"Then we'll come up with something else."

She looked at him for a long time, and he felt her looking

at him tenderly, that for the first time in his life she was looking at him tenderly.

"Don't you get cold?" she asked quietly.

"Sometimes, but it'll be warmer together."

She thought about something for a rather long time and
suddenly smiled.

"I've been so lost the last few weeks. Absolutely. Literally."

"You'll tell me all about it."

"Maybe."

And he realized she was here to stay. And that this was the
beginning of their life.

Opposite the barrier with the red light the streetlamps were
already lit. The barrier was raised and people had begun stream-
ing out. A gramophone started playing in the café where the
carnival dwarves and the bearded lady gathered to warm up at
the zinc bar. At half past eight there was supposed to be a performance starting on the square.

A rope was strung up to mark off the stage; a worn rug had
been spread on the cobblestones in the middle and the dumb-
bells put out for the crudely made-up athlete. A clown was
walking his trained dogs. The crowd would begin gathering at
around eight o'clock. Taking advantage of the fact that people
would get bored waiting, Misha Sergeich's friend came with his
guitar, sat down on a box, and in his gypsy voice sang:

> *I have a mustache,*
> *Marusia has her braids.*
> *Our life will pass for nothing:*
> *Down the same highway.*
> *I have a mustache,*